NEW-CLASSIC SCIENC[
BOOK FIVE

Further Yet

TREVOR WATTS

Further Yet Copyright © 2021 by Trevor Watts.

All rights reserved. No part of this book may be reproduced in any form or by any electronic or mechanical means including information storage and retrieval systems, without permission in writing from the author. The only exception is by a reviewer, who may quote short excerpts in a review.

This book is a work of fiction. Names, characters, places, and incidents either are products of the author's imagination or are used fictitiously. Any resemblance to actual persons, living or dead, events, or locales is entirely coincidental. The illustrations were all created by the author or adapted from free-to-download, or paid-for, images from the internet. Four of the stories have been included in the Giant SF Anthology "Of Other Times and Spaces".

Dedicated to Chris Watts
For her editing skills, commitment and tolerance.

Log on to https://www.sci-fi-author.com/
Facebook at Creative Imagination

First Printing: 2021
Brinsley Publishing Services

ISBN: 9798680570425

CONTENTS

NOT EXACTLY	1
EXPERIENCE	3
HE REALLY SHOULDN'T	9
IT'S IN MI DRAWERS	21
I'M WORKING ON THAT	25
SURVIVE THE NIGHT	29
WITH A WILL OF HER OWN	73
THE GALAXY'S GREATEST CRIMINAL.	77
THE SECRET OF VONDUR'EYE	83
CONTROL	89
SCABBY	95
I WAS JUST COMING TO THAT	161
DON'T ASK	165
COUPLA YUMANS	173
SHIMMER	181
ALL FOR ONE	189
DO YOU HEAR WHAT I HEAR?	195
ABOUT THE AUTHOR	205
BY THE SAME AUTHOR	206
A FEW NOTES	214

NOT EXACTLY

'Species?' I heard the voice, somewhere above me in the hovering blackness...

'Human,' I heard that as well. *Who's speaking? Are they speaking, or am I just hearing them within?*

'Alive?' The tone sounded more tick-off-enquiry tone than concerned.

Something poked me – my chest. *I'm lying down?*

I remember. We were fighting. Our combat group – eight humans and two helmish scouts – was in a skirmish against a troop of ghasres we'd ambushed. We had every intention of wiping them out – except for a couple to spit-roast and eat, and a couple for the interrogators.

Another poke. In my ribs this time. 'Yes, it's alive.'

My eyes are opening. Swirling dark stinking smoke writhing round.

But they were a decoy group, heavily armed; with triple the numbers we expected. I'd been hit and gone down, ferocious hand-to-claw fighting all round me. In and out of consciousness; I couldn't move a muscle.

Something looming and moving. Coming closer, clearer. Huge eyes. A face. It's a ghasre. Smiling to expose razor-teeth, warm eyes – hot eyes, near glowing. It wavered and reformed like a spirit-wraith... as if tuning itself to my vision. 'Oh, God,' I said.

'Not exactly,' the words came to me. The face was still reforming – the eyes becoming brighter red, gleaming hard. The smile broadening to a grimace that split, revealing reddened teeth… as sharp as the claws that were forming…

'Not God,' it said. 'In fact, quite the opposite.'

EXPERIENCE

'So how'd you get here? And why?'

I glanced up from my present case, finishing up with some medication and dressings. *Ah, here's someone new.*

He'd brought a casualty in from out of town, currently being processed at the outer triage unit. It would take ten minins to do that. Someone had mentioned the duty-doc was through here, so he'd wandered through the exxo ward to find me. For a chatter, it seemed, before I attended to his casualty.

It would take just as long for me to finish with this one, so I wasn't displeased at the opportunity to speak with someone new, 'Me? I came out here in 42, from Maikleen. It was here or the reintegration vat.'

I nodded to Moynee to finish up, and left her to it.

'You? The reintegration vat? You're not serious?'

'No,' I laughed, 'Not entirely; they're a mite beyond that, but not far off.'

He seemed to be interested, and he was someone new, so I carried on, always happy to chat with anyone I hadn't met before. 'Yes, I screwed up a diagnosis. I thought it was a weevil borehole that had gone septic, but it turned out to be a rad-shot through the head.'

He looked incredulous that anyone could make such a clang.

No time for that now – Yeuk, my hands were gunged-up. I sluiced them under the taps, 'I got the blame – naturally. They were all teeth and claws about it, and wouldn't listen to my side, so I headed this way

– colony planet on the furthest fringe of the Humanic Realm at the time. This planet was ideal for me, with hardly any contact with Central Gov.

Looking round, yes, this place suits me fine; always has done. 'I got a job here, pretty much the same as I would have had on Perritt, and more freedom to do as I wanted. The patients are all humans, so no strife with mis-diagnoses. Yoigers, but that was a trying time.'

'As Full Doc?' He started rinsing his own hands.

'Sure. What else? I had all the memo-drops; and they'd had time to bed in and mature in my brain; plus training experience for three years.'

'You'd already had all that? And you still fruckled up a diagnosis?'

'Yeah, well, I was human-only trained. All my experience and learning was that way. I know my fellow human beings forwards, backwards and inside-out. I was good. Glittering career was looming for me somewhere. All the new colonies sprouting on fifty different planets. Isolated settlements crying out for a resident doc.'

'And?' He was looking at his wet hands. I pointed to the air-blast button.

'It was my final term on Perritt and I'm on a travelling tour to get extra experience of different ailments and injuries – you know – deep-sea-men, foresters, miners, engineers, chemic workers… whatever was thrown at us, really.'

'And?'

'Eighth day out, I'm called to an incident on the superway. "High impact incident." That was all I was told. I get there and I'm into this unit that's a bit crumpled, expecting some guy with bones broken, bleeding, whatever. Maybe multiple casualties, and I'm all psyched-up and I've run a re-memo through my head on the way over. Just to freshen up my memory, you know. Should be a valuable learning experience…'

'And?'

'He's bleeding, alright – green watery blood from a gash in his carapace, and trickling down one of his faces – I think that's what they were.'

'Shit.'

'Yes, that, too.'

'So it all went pear-shaped?'

'He was pear-shaped to start with – but by then, he'd gone more like a corkscrew-shaped cactus. There was a clear hole, black, with a scoured edge – classic bore-weevil. They can land and start grinding in without you being aware if you're busy, like fully occupied with driving a rapidex unit. Or you might notice, but can't reach… or the anaesthetic they exude numbs you to the event. So, anyway, that's what I thought had caused the off-route crash.

'What the fruckle was it?'

We started heading for the admissions section where his charge would be.

'Two of them, Heprocids; visitors from the other side of the inward fringe. I patched him up – probed for the weevil – nothing I could detect, so I sealed his cracks, re-set four legs or arms or whatevers.

'There was no advisory help for me, and he didn't have any companions there to tell me any different; and no connections with the stellar-mesh to get a third opinion on him. Then I saw the additional fracture points under the sub-wing Malpighian nodules, and realised there was more to this. Eventually, I extracted a couple of needle bolts and sealed the impact points. I thought I'd done okay.'

We had to wait aside for a moment as a self-guide pallet of supplies drifted along the corridor, not paying much attention to where it was going.

'The on-spot guys showed me the corpse of the other one, smashed-up in the back of the unit, and it all came out. It seemed the hole wasn't a weevil: it was a 42T rad bolt. They were assumed to have been fighting, or playing, or something. They'd probably both fired… the unit crashed, rolled and smashed itself up.'

'But… your misdiagnosis of the cause of the hole didn't make any difference, did it? You sealed it, patched him for in-house treatment?'

'Yep, pretty, neat, too.'

'But?'

'It seems that injured Heprocids have to leak a huge mass of body fluids out; the green plasma. Their bodies produce excess haemo and it has to re-set its own balance…'

'So, basically?'

'I poisoned him by sealing in all the tainted fluids. He wasn't quite dead. I didn't fail my Passout, but they told me I'd never get a job on Perritt until I had a *lot* more experience with non-humanic species. The Hepros were coming in greater numbers – tourists, traders, settlers, and I was stamp-marked as non-kopo. So it wouldn't do to have me around.'

We were approaching the triage unit, 'So, let me guess,' he almost dared to laugh, 'you headed in the opposite direction to avoid any chance of contact with them again. You sure came far enough, eh?'

'Certainly hope so. Haven't seen hide or carapace of them since. I've been four years here, up to my neck in broken bones and burst bowels, viruses and varicose veins; plus three hundred other gruesome, but purely humanic, problems.'

'Yes, the staff in Triage said you were making good. Thriving, huh?'

'Not too bad; on-going learning, of course – still need more experience. This's a relatively new environment, illnesses, the occasional radiation bursts. The diets – sheesh! The stuff some people eat out here. Anyway, what's with this one you called me for?'

'He had an accident in the fish-processing plant the other side of Western Lake.'

'Bad?'

'Two tentacles trapped in the machinery, nearly ripped off; excurrent siphonal canal crushed; labial ganglion's badly twis—'

'Oh, shit.'

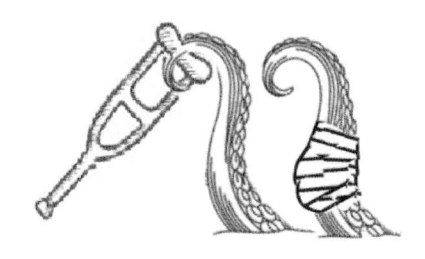

HE REALLY SHOULDN'T

Sometimes, you look round at what you've walked into, and you wonder if you've done the right thing. But you consider the alternatives, get your head down, and make the best of it, right?

The aft cargo hold of the space trader Tekan Kana was a pit of that nature. *Tie your hair back, girl; tighten your bra; and be glad of the ride.*

But after a walk-through, looking for crew quarters, I decided it was more like a *PIT*, actually – capital letters, gold embossed and neon-lit. Not only the decaying, leaky hull plates and recesses of filth and vermin, but the work boss was a total shiker, too. He was bad. Nasty, even for a bristleback from Jikee. Yes, that Jikee – bigger than we humans, with keratin bodies and chitin externals. It's a weird insect-crabby body mix; and their minds are just as twisted – more akin to killer shraks than us.

With Boss Yorger, that attitude was all there in blades. And he let the crew know it with his bullying. Within five minins of coming aboard, I had the hold-crew telling me all about him...

'He's invincible – look at the size of him—'

'He's a big sucker, this one—'

'And he *is* a sucker – *two* proboscises – he's a head taller than any human.' So that's around two heads taller than me.

All the guys moaned about him, and regaled me and the other newcomer with tales of what we had coming, now we were in the black hole of the Tekan Kana's after-hold. 'All dim lighting, low oxy level and a threat round every corner,' as a pair of avvies told us before they even showed us the bunks and feed bar.

I looked at Boss Yorger anew – wearing a tight-fit alloy coverall that made him doubly impregnable.

'So he knows he'll get away with his bullying? Nothing to stop him?'

You ever seen an avvie shrug? All their top feathers ruffle in sequence. 'He gets the essentials done – cargoes loaded and unloaded swiftly, regardless of the conditions or safety issues.'

'We lost two crew last trip—' The beaky crew were all chattering then. Trying to warn me, or just scare me, I dunno.

'He was over-hurrying and din't fill their tanks up with enough oxy. 'Course, he's the only one who can check the gauges—'

'Might have been deliberate: they didn't get on.'

'So he gets away with it every time. The master, and the owners don't care – we're only itinerants... illegals on the dodge from somebody or something.'

Boss Yorger was the only discussion in the off-break after my first shift – the one that lasted two shifts, but only counted as one. It made for depressing listening, so I stuck an ear-pod in, and immersed in Ultra-peace – the Senya collection. I'd rather be calm and relaxed inside with her music, than all roiled up with their whinging and pointless plotting.

'Look, guys, I'm unchallenging, insignificant. He probably hasn't noticed me. I do my whack; no reason to pick on—'

'He don't need a reason,' one of the plumed avvies said. 'He enjoys it. And we're *all* bullied. He'll get you.'

'It ain't only him – he's lead-gaffer of four fellow bristlebacks who follow him round, enforcing his orders with snidey digs and pokes of their blackjo prods.' They were all nodding and touching at tender bits.

The rest of us – fourteen humans and eight avvies – the ones with long crest feathers – were the gang, the work force. The work entailed loading and reloading when we were in dock at some orbit station or cargo transfer depot. That much was standard and obvious.

'And when we're in travel time, Yorger keeps us slaving at re-balancing, cleaning, de-lousing—'

'And taking all the risks with poison-teeth vermin, dirty air, polluted water—'

'And a beating whenever he's bored, or takes a dislike to someone—'

'Or a liking to what they've got. He sliced my case open on my first trip... and my top crest when I complained.' That was from one the avvies who can whine out the nostrils at the base of his beak. Awesome when he's in full whinging mode – neck feathers out at right angles, quivering like vibro-sealers fixing the hull plating.

'Virtually unpaid, too. The pay package is nudging the zero line.'

'Look,' I pulled my music ear pod out. 'You don't like it, so why the nork are you aboard? Why put yourselves in his bludgeon line?'

They all claimed to have different reasons, 'Working our passage around the Federation and Commonwealth territories, now they're at peace of a kind.'

'It's an adventure.'

'I'm on the dodge. They can't track me aboard this crate.'

'You haven't seen my wife.'

'It's the only free way to travel around the Cygnus Spiral Arm, seeing the sights, looking for work.'

'And this Yorger guy's taking full advantage of his position, and our vulnerability? So why do you keep moaning in my direction? What the nork has it got to do with me? I'm the new hand on my first leg aboard this ship. Inoffensive... humanic female. He hasn't affected me yet, so I'm not joining in with your chuntering and plotting.'

I wasn't even listening to most of it. I pull my weight, and plenty more besides – I'm only small, but I'm lean and I can look after myself if any of the guys decides to get amorous. I stuck my music pod back in.

Except, he *will* pick on me one shift, before long. And when he's had a go, his cronies'll feel free to do the same. So maybe I'd better take some avoiding action before too long.

Boss Yorger – all double-weight and double-size of him, plus shiny carapace and glittery eyes – went through the other new guy's belongings on the third shift, stole his gold cord bracelet and his cash creds. Course, all the crew were complaining, especially the new guy – he was bitter and raving. And a couple of the avvies were affronted that Yorger had ripped out a pincerful of their crest feathers to decorate his cubicle.

That seemed a touch extreme, even to me, but the avvies were dire about it. For the sort with the long crests, it was as bad as it gets, like being raped. 'Being plucked is being fucked', as they say.

I mean, I've worked with avvies quite a bit, and they're not shell-back toughies like Yorger and his Jikee crew, any more than we humans are. They're particularly jittery and fragile-boned; same as we're rather vulnerable to auto-pincers – it's our soft flesh and brittle bones that are our downfall that way. Razor serrations on diamond-hard pincers beat a jugular artery every time.

I watched him. He glanced my way a couple of times. They have this way of smiling: the jaws ease apart and quiver. *He's going to get me in the next day or two, and/or raid my stash. Yeah, a definite tell there – brief glitter from one compound eye. A set of little facets focusing my way. He's coming for me soon.*

I'd prefer he didn't.

The work-crew complained and whinged as soon as we came off-shift, right from the first in-flight shift after our launch towards Kalèdas. It's a twenty-day trip, so they got a lot of whining to get through. Workwise, there was actually plenty to do – retightening cargo, plugging leaks, overhauling the loading mechanism, vermin-catching... endless. Plus the travellers' mug – gambling in the off-times.

Skok knows why, but they all kept looking at me when they moaned, like they expected *me* to do something about it.

'Look. I'm new. He an't touched me. I'm the littlest here. I'm a lady.' They all had the nerve to look dubious about that. 'So get out my hair.'

But would they chuff? On and on they went. 'Okay, okay,' I said, thoroughly pussed up with their incessant buffing about it, 'I'll speak with Yorger. Next shift. See if he can be more reasonable about things.'

'Yeah, right...'

'You and whose navy?'

'What makes you think you can—?'

'Me? Well, you know...' I rolled over on my strapdown. 'It's got to happen sometime – might as well get it over.'

'Gonna let him give you a dobbing, rob your bags, and hope it ain't too bad, huh?'

'Seen kids like you before... all mouth and slimy guts.'

'Kay... kay...' I sat up. 'If that's how you see me, why the fungal Boo do you keep whining at me? Look at yourselves – there you all stand, sit and perch. You're a gang of scruffs, workers, hard guys, avvies down on their tails, but you're all looking at me, like you just exposed me as the BigMouth from Orbit 4. I an't said a word for or against Yorger. I don't care about him. Got plenty else on my mind.'

'You just look like you imagine you know better than everybody else, looking down on us.'

Sarky skugger. It's Big Beaky who looks down on everybody, if only because he's a head taller than any of us. 'Right,' I said. 'I look down on *you?* From down here? I'm the littly, remember? out the whole bunch of us.' Didn't do me any good – they just looked like it was me who was next, so I had to be the one to thwart Yorger's plans.

'Yeah, okay. I told you I'd go talk with him. Just leave me be, huh?'

But would they chuffaslike? 'And what the skug makes you think you got the woosy to so much as speak to Boss Yorger?'

'*Come on!* You go on at me to do something. And when I say I will, you go on even more.' Story time, I decided. 'Okay, guys, okay. I'll tell you a little story, and you leave me in peace, okay?'

They sort of settled for that, still all acting stupid like it was my fault. 'When I was a kid on Havand, I had six brothers. I was the only girl, and the youngest out the pack. And, even for a girl, I was well smaller than average.'

'Y' still are.' They laughed; a bit derisive.

Get on with it, I'm accustomed to ignorance from the eight different alien species plus humans I've come across. You're no different. 'My brothers, they bullied the shike out of me. Merciless, they were. Dad shrugged, cos he was under mum's heel, and probably thought they were doing the world a favour by tormenting the vulnerable female in the family. So I put up with it, till one day my oldest brother Jaydeen, gave me a right slapping round, and my face swelled up like an Arseen pudding, and I could hardly breathe.'

'So what? What's that got—'

His mouth stopped. I can put on that kind of stare sometimes. 'I knew they'd kill me if things carried on like that – I was eight years old, Havand-year counting. So I went to a training gym and asked'em to toughen me up.

'Thirty-six days working myself to a frazzle, and we all decided I wasn't getting any stronger, bigger or better, and if I kept doing it, I still wouldn't become ferocious enough to sort out my brothers, and I'd be dead by End-Fall.'

'Yeah, right, so what?'

'I went to the toughest guy in the place – guy called Thug. He was small, too, about the size I am now. And I asked him, "How come you do what you like? They're all scared of you."

'He laughed, and was saying, "We got something in common, eh? You have to summon up all your hard times and your hatings. Bring them all up inside you, focus them. You have to be prepared to put *everything* into it – far more than them. I'd kill any of them any time. I'm gutter-born and I learned the hard way. They all know I mean exactly what I say."'

'And you're going for Yorger based on that?' Huh – newly bald avvie interrupting me.

'Going for him? No. I only said I'd speak to him – big difference. I trust he'll see things my way. My brothers did, when I beat the living shike out of Jaydeen, and would have killed him if he hadn't cried the bleat. He knew I could have doubled him up, so he really meant it when he licked the dish. I took his place, organised the others better than he had, and never had to threaten them again. Sure, they still hated me, but they were richer and more respected than before, so they let it continue.'

'And you think—?'

'Cos you beat up a little boy—'

'You believe you can take on a bristleback Jikee the size and strength of Yorger?'

'Yeah, well, you know…' I shrugged. 'I'm not taking him on; I'll talk to him about it.'

I was good entertainment for the rest of the off-shift – not for the pistle-taking, but I can play the Sarrit fingercord pretty well, and know lots of songs from more'n a dozen planets. I finished up with 'Spacers' Lament', so that had'em all weepy eyed sad as shit when they turned in.

I decided to have a few words with Boss Yorger next shift when we trooped into the liquids hold to do some spillage control. There he stood, at the bulkhead door, built like a crabsect with plating, checking us in. He gave me a look, fixed on me, so I knew he had something up his carapace for me.

I get four light-grav steps past him... quick look back...he's facing the other way, watching the last three coming in behind me. I spun and took a running leap, was on his back, sending him crashing down on the steel plating, forcing my fist under him and jamming an electrobolt through the division in his gorgelet plates into his throat. Rammed it in and gave him a solid tronic blast to let him know I was serious.

One proboscis ripped off and the other twisted in a fist-grip, and he was helpless. His pincers couldn't grip that close in, and he was almost paralysed with another electrobolt zap inside his pharynx. So he wouldn't say much for a while, either. I had a few words in his shell-like, on his preferences between life doing what I told him for the next twenty-plus days, or an agonising lectro-death with an airlock exit before shift's end.

We had an agreement, just like that. Okay, so it was more than just a few words. They included a good bit of electro punctuation.

He agreed, and he meant it. He saw the error of his ways. He would never beat or pinch anyone again; he would return the gold bracelet and the plumage.

Just like the other people in the gym were with Thug, he knew I would do precisely what I said. It came to him that I was insane, and utterly vicious. So I was best given in to, or he wouldn't live through the shift. Much as the electro-bolter and I explained once or twice more.

Things improved after that. Immediately, actually. Yorger kept his second proboscis; the lost one would regenerate; and he still had one compound eye.

He was well enough to return to work after two shifts, but by then his four underlings and the general work crew had buckled-in as well, and tightened-down some loose cargo, cleaned out two alcoves and exterminated a nest of rayts. All done in record time. No injuries. No arguing. All for extra nectar, nuts or alccoll, depending on the species, and we were all set.

'You letting him back in?'

'Sure, he might think about coming for me. But he won't do anything. And the others sure won't. You best make certain he understands his new place – I an't staying aboard the Tekan Kana forever.'

'And this is just from what you did to your brothers? Years ago?'

I checked the seals on the hull plates that we'd just repaired and looked round the little group of beakies, skinnies and shellies. 'Okay, I'm not the sort to lie about such things. The guy, Thug, in the gym, when he was saying about summoning up all his hate and focus, he reached in his pocket and said, "You also need *this* in one hand..." That was the electrobolt. "And *this* in the other."'

'Yeah, what was that?' Somewhat disbelieving, the sceptics wanted to know.

'A dose of androphate.'

'Andro what—?' The de-crested avvies didn't know about warp-drugs. Not many people do.

'Gives you an edge: you're faster and more vicious than anything else alive. And the electrobolt gives you the means to make sure you get whatever it is you've demanded.'

The looks on their faces. 'You keep them with you all the time?'

'A locket round my neck. Here... see? One touch on the pad pumps a mill of andro straight into me; and the electrobolt is up my sleeve.' I slipped it down into my grip, turned it over, and slid it back.

It was like they saw me in a whole new light; some new realisation. Bit slow, they were.

'It's not the first time you've done this kind of thing, is it?'

I don't know what it is, but I just sort of unburden now and again, especially when there's eff'all they can do about it. So I kinda confessed, 'Er... well, did you hear about President Lijj on Pentill?'

'Pentill? Where you joined us?'

'What about him? He was assassinated, a few days before we landed there.'

'Middle of the Tri-planet conference.'

'Professional hit, they said. Between the eye stalks.' I gained the impression they were edging away.

'What are you saying? You had something to do with that? You?'

It was a bit embarrassing, really. 'I should'a known – the money was too good. It was four high-business avvies who hired me. No, not avvies like you: they were the smooth-head-fluffy-tailed lot from Graudgierr. They refused to pay me afterwards; tipped off the law, and thought I'd be quick-caught and killed. I tell you, I do the job exactly as they specify, ultra-efficient, and they're stupid enough to think they're gonna screw me up.'

'So?'
'You plucked'em?'
'Scorched'em?
'Thieved'em blind?'

'Ha – you know me too well already. So soon.' I smiled all round, just quiet-like, and left it at that. Let them think what they want, believe what they like.

The business avvies on Pentill? I did all three – plucked'em, scorched'em and robbed'em to the bone.

Four featherless and spot-burned corpses later, and I knew the intricacies of their premises, and the code for their safe. I helped myself to the copious cash contents, counting them as my contract payment, plus generous bonuses.

Never mind the five deaths back on Pentill, I had eighteen million good reasons why I *really* didn't want Boss Yorger raiding my gear.

IT'S IN MI DRAWERS

'Ay up, yon drawer just shut its sen.'

I'm in the back of my garage in the extension I built, like a workshop where I can do all my fixing things and building, adapting and repairs and all that. Okay, so it's a bit of a pit-heap and there's junk everywhere. Except, of course, it in't all junk, it's my stuff and tools that I know and love and use – most of it. Course, some of it, I don't use every day... and it clutters up t'bench and't shelves and under't bench and everywhere.

But I'm not having summat come shuttin't drawers just like that when I'm getting stuff out on'em all't time.

I'm doing a bit of maintenance on't trailer, cos I'm off camping in't South o' France at weekend, and I've got to put wheels back on and check brakes and all that.

And the set of drawers under't bench – they're easy places to dump things off the bench – like mi spanners and screwdriver and wheel nuts for't trailer. It's dead simple just to open the end drawer and hand-sweep stuff into it – out o' sight and all that, and then I know where't stuff is f't trailer next time I need it. There's four drawers in a row – plus a couple o' tea chests for the big stuff. Like mi tent and pegs and cooking stuff and all that gubbins.

That drawer, end'n on't left, were solid stuck when I started this morning. Had to prise it open wi't big driver from mi toolbox. And I'm getting started on't trailer when I hear this sliding noise, and't drawer's just shut its sen.

Well, I mean. What d'y'do?

I went over and pulled it back open, got the grease gun out, and a pair o' pliers and left it open agen.

There's something in there. It pulled the drawer back shut. Drawers don't do that on their own.

So I propped it open wi' a spanner. I'm getting on wi't job, and't spanner goes flying up in't air, and drawer's shut its sen agen.

Right. If it's war then. I got a brick and shoved it in, dead solid wedge, that was. And I outstared it. Ten bloody minutes, it took, but it did it! Brick suddenly comes hurtling up in't air and practically through't ceiling o' mi garage.

Right, I'm throwing caution t' wind now, and I pulled it open and shouted in, 'Whoever you are. Come on out.' I kept hold of it, till I felt it tremble, and I didn't want to lose mi fingers, so I let go. And I'm kneeling there shouting back in't drawer again. 'You shut y'sen agen and I'll take this to y'.' And I held mi circular power saw and gave it a quick burst – teeth ripping into't edge o't bench top – I usually do that by accident. 'It'll have this thing apart in no time,' I warned it. 'Then you'll have nowhere to live. So come on out. Show thi'sens.'

So I'm waiting for like half a minute and I give it another buzz and a quick rip at the top edge. There's all this noise, and sawdust flying in all directions. I give it a rest and shout, 'Are you coming out then?' And there's like a little shuffling noise inside. And it's not words I know, but I'm getting them in mi head and it's saying like, 'We are the mighty Arakka. Do not attempt to interfere with us.'

'What y doing here?' I asked.

'This is our base.'

'What? Back o' my garage?'

'This is merely the beginning.' This voice, sounding like a cross between the Emperor Ming and Betty who runs chippy on't corner.

'Beginning o' what?'

'World domination.'

'Well, that's a laugh for a start. Summat little, using my set o' drawers in back o' mi garage? Daren't even show y' sens.' I laughed and give the saw another quick buzz, to reassure misen and put frighteners on 'em a bit more. Thought I saw something glittering in there. *Is it eyes or a super-weapon?* I asked mi sen.

'World domination? Tha's starting in't wrong place for that, tha knows. Our Arthur tried it – Young Scargill, and look where it got him. No-bloody-wheer.'

There was silence. I lowered the buzz saw – big heavy Parkside one from Lidl, it is. I cut mi sen with it once, nearly had mi thumb off. Besides, I din't really want to chop mi bench up. 'What you got in there? Mother mutant mouse? No? Spaceship, is it?'

The silence seemed a mite negative. 'No spaceship, huh? Been abandoned? Or – it occurred to me, 'is it a time and space portal gate you're setting up?'

'A what?' comes back at me.

'Ahh, so you're on your own, are you?'

Bit of an awkward silence. Then it… or they… come out wi' it agen, 'We seek World Domination.'

'Course you do,' I said. 'But this in't the place fo' thi to be starting, like I said. It's cowd'n'wet here all t' time round here. No… what you want is somewhere warm and sunny to get y' sens started.'

'Oh?' comes this querying thought wave from t' drawer.

'Aye, where you need to be is South of France.

Silence again. 'I can show y't brochures, if y' like. Or if you can peek inside mi 'ed? Aye – ooh, y' can.'

So I started having thoughts about South of France from last couple o' years – sun, sea, palm trees, vin plonk, this French bird I met— *Not there.* I warned them off that bit, and I'm getting all these warm thoughts about the idea.

'The people there? Are they hard, determined fighters?'

'The French? Gimme a laugh. *The French?* Nah, everybody pushes them round. Us, and't Germans do, anyroad. Bit of a shove and a threat and they roll ovver, every time. Least bit of an invasion – y'know. Owt from Leeds United up t' Germans. Tha's'll be all raight theer.

Tell y' what – I'm going camping down that way at weekend – I could give thee a lift, if tha fancies?'

I'M WORKING ON THAT

'You look fabulous,' I said. 'I could almost go for you myself.' I walked round her, studying with well-practised eyes – another very attractive naked woman. I stroked the right buttock – pressed. Very nicely firm. Breasts? Yes, very pert. 'And – just checking my dear – Yes, beautifully firm. That's one aspect I'm working on.' Stepping back to appraise – and, yes, to admire.

'Okay – turn around... nice, yes, and walk to the statue over there... and turn... return... Perfect; nice, light step, hip rotation not too obvious. I'm working on that, too.'

'Right, Revert Eleven-nine-six-two. Now.

'Oh, yes. Smoothly done.' She re-melded to her native form in five-point two seconds. Pretty good for a Newbie. A little shorter and fatter than the average human form, but the same overall mass, of course, even though she had two tentacle pairs for grasping, and three more pairs for locomotion. Very shiny, almost looking slimy, but that's the natural protective cream they exude in the sunlight here. The front and rear eyes looked uncertain – perhaps for my approval. But it hardly mattered what I thought of my clients' original species-form – perfectly suited for life on Solucan, where they live in submarine cities that stretch from the oceanic ooze to well above the stormy surface. I've visited a few times, familiarising myself, setting up a local office, recruiting, satisfying the increasing demand to come to the humanic planet ofAarde. Personally, I prefer *their* planet. The Sea-Garden Planet of Solucan, I call it.

Much nicer than the neurops' home planet, for instance – far too dry and rocky for my liking, but they're actually my biggest customers, in more ways than one, and good payers, too. Took a lot of work to adapt the technology to enable the neurops to become Aarde-like beings. But some are really keen to come and settle on here – in desert-fringe settlements, naturally.

'Okay, fine, my dear. And now, reform human... Ah yes.' I've been working on the speed and accuracy of reformation – at one time a few of them became stuck in halfway stages, but that was embarrassing for everyone concerned. Even after all this time on the job, I'm still improving myself and working on new methods, tweaking old ones, working on various aspects. 'Let's check you again.' I inspected her once more.

Finally, I was satisfied that she could consistently re-form perfectly, into an identical human pattern at first attempt, within ten seconds. By the end of the morning session, she did it easily.

'Try the walk again... Fine... and the smile. Lovely.

'You want to try some other variations? Okay – longer hair... Beautiful – looks nice. No – not down there as well; not that long, anyway. Just the head.

'I think three pairs of breasts is overdoing it just a touch. Yes, really. It might well attract the wrong kind of attention, and isn't at all common among humans, here on Aarde. How about you try the hips slightly wider? Yes, lovely... narrower waist... Beautiful. Larger breasts... er... Maybe not quite so— *No! Too much.* We have too many like that on Aarde already.

'Right... next, let's go over the language embedment.' That's another area I'm working on, especially smoothing out the slightly earthy accent some Solucans seem to have. Fluency… phraseology… recognising meanings and intentions by tone of voice. And your own tones of voice in conversation. Serious, laugh, meek. 'Oooh – too commanding.'

It took the rest of the day to go over her systems and functions. It'll be at least one more full day checking the knowledge packs and memories are well embedded. And sex – there'll be at least one bout of that. Often more – it can be exhausting, but I'm working on the stamina and performance aspects.

'There'll be plenty of chance for that later.' I have to insist on not too much at once. 'It depends who you choose to be, or to accompany, or if you want to be semi-independent.'

I have to keep some check and monitoring on them throughout the whole beginning of the introductory phase here. They need to experience sex at least once before being allowed out. The Solucans can't cross-reproduce – not humanic-looking offspring, anyway. But I'm working on that.

And their contracts… Ten years seems a long time to have on-going support, but that's the idea, for them to be really accustomed to life on Aarde, thoroughly embedded, naturalised. Then when their contract is up, they can choose to revert to their natural form, and continue their present lives, but as Solucans. Or simply carry on as they are, living as apparently full humans. Whether staying on Aarde or returning to Solucan, they'll have the choice; or they can even come in for a self-redesign, completely new shape. But that's something to face in the future, I've only been doing this for seven years. I tell you, I need a rest.

I imagine that Aarde is going to be mildly surprised when the first tranche of Solucans appears among the population, and the native humans find they've been playing host to around a thousand wonderfully-integrated alien ladies.

What the general intention is among the Solucans, I really don't know; I've been working on gathering some consumer feedback before the first contracts are up, see how many are thinking of retaining their human form or reverting to Solucan. Or a fluid combination could work, I expect, especially as their tentacles really are very smart.

With only three years to go before any members of the first group can reveal themselves, perhaps I ought to be working on finding out what they might need thereafter – guidance, reassurance, sex – Solucan-style – or an occasional evening reminiscing about the tides and currents of home.

But yes, it could be very interesting in three years' time. As one of the very first featherines, from Avianna, I've trained myself in all the human foibles and habits, from picking my nose to scratching my balls, I might even "come out" myself.

Now that *would* cause a bit of a flap.

SURVIVE THE NIGHT

'Xuday. If you're listening up there, let me survive one more night. You can do that, hmm?' I re-tightened my seat strapping, and clamped the lap and neck braces down. 'Jecksy. Tighten your froiking belt down.'

No point letting him seduce me if he's going to kill himself in this stupid slow-motion accident. He heaved at the straps obediently.

Looking out the glassite curved window, there seemed little chance of surviving much longer. But then, fourteen out the last fifteen nights had loomed pretty much the same. On the other hand, being half way down a slow-moving landslide, sideways-on, plus lots of screeching from the carriage and the other passengers was even less confidence-building than previous nights.

'Yiihhh!!! Shikes!' The bus slid another couple of lengths down the precipitous rock face. Perfectly sideways now.

Nine nights ago, we'd lost the first carriage out the convoy, struggling up a slippery slope and pushing the engine too much. It had overheated, exploded and blown the whole vehicle to radioactive smidds. Messy. But at least it got rid of that whining Doods family with their repulsive progeny and that lecherous guard.

'Oh! Shoiks!' Another grinding sideways skid, ending in a near-rollover when we came up against a rock or something. 'Shikes!! We'll go right over next time.'

Leaning…
More…
More…

Creaking and grinding.

It's sky out the window my side now – thirty or forty degrees over. *Not much further before we go...*

Two nights after the Doods' grand exit, it was the rear vehicle that didn't make it to the midday rendezvous. We backtracked. The rear end of its roof was just visible sticking out the Gloy-swamp that we'd skirted round. Well, I wasn't going in a swamp ever again, especially not to look for my two my louse-ridden brothers who'd been aboard that one – pestering some new girls, no doubt. No loss.

I almost hoped our shoiking carriage would roll – it'd really give this lot something to shriek about – before it shut them up for good. *Maybe if I bounce up and down a bit. Get my boobs bouncing in time – that'd give Jecksy the Lech something more to drool over.*

Which left only two vehicles still trekking across the Cursed Plateau – actually, it's the Corrig-haar Plateau on Andronor, but it *is* cursed. Heading towards the Promised Resettlement Lands – or The Hurrogg Flats, as the map said. *We got Fat-boy's chance of arriving there at this rate of attrition. Half the convoy gone the way of the wind already.*

As I'd predicted, yesterday took its toll, too. Our sole remaining companion bus went the way of the locals. It'd broken down, and they all climbed out to wander round – when they were attacked by a pack of marauding Hongos with whip-teeth. What do we have guards for, if they're going to debark the bus, and start chatting the passengers up, instead of shoiking guarding them?

And, following the Hongos like a murmuration was a trillion poison-biting insects. I don't know – or much care – which bunch they succumbed to. But they were all dead within the hour.

'We ain't opening our doors to'em,' Soldeen the Randy Driver declared as we approached the body-and insect-strewn site. 'We'd go the same way.' So we left them there – drove over a few on the way, I think, where they'd collapsed. Felt the wheels bump and squelch over a few lumps of something, anyway.

A jerk. Lurch. Grinding. 'Hold yekking tight!' I yelled at Jecksy. 'We're going over.'

Renewed screeching from vehicle and passengers. The carriage leaned more and more – *Check the straps, girl* – the ground under us still shifting.

And over we went in a slow roll. Up up uuuuupppp and over with a massive shattering crash. *One rollover ain't the end of this. Slope's too steep. Too much momentum. We're headed for the bottom of this cliff.* I crushed my head down as low as I could get – saw Jecksy do the same, neck brace and all. *Xuday-alone knows what the rest are up to – or how far it is to the base of this slope. Don't suppose we'll find out. Ain't going to survive this.*

Over again, faster... Pandemonium hardly came into it – utter crashing and screaming everywhere. I'm jolted like I'm a scraggle-doll. Again a roll... Arms flailing and screams piercing everywhere. Glassite smashing in. Another... Side-struts caving and bending. Again... again... Roof crushed and buckled... then tearing away.

Definitely on a roll here, I thought, between neck-breaking jerks. A rock splattered the man in front of me

– upside-down at the time, I think. It never ended – it still wrecks and jolts in my mind, waking or sleeping.

Ears splitting and body battered, the movement ceased, after one more slow, rolling drop-over.

Took me some long time to think into my compulsive survival prayer – must be getting jipped-off with the sound of my voice just lately. 'Thanks, Xuday. Another chance, huh?' Not that I was too confident about it – *maybe I'm critically injured; or trapped; or fire'll spread; or the night-freeze will be—* 'Come on, Xuday. Just let me survive one more night, huh?'

Story of my brief, underclass life, that was – day to day survival. *Get through another night, girl. Just survive.*

We were more upside than rightside, smashed apart and the cold was intense already. All that moaning and crying. *Why do they need to do that? If I can move, I'm coming round you with a blade.*

It was an even longer time to free myself from the straps, braces, crushed-back seats, two bodies and one soon-to-be-a-body-at-the-rate-she-was-whining. Shoik – it was a mess. Most of the passengers hadn't bothered with straps or braces, so they'd bounced round with extreme violence. And half had been thrown out and strewn down the rocky face above us.

As events were going just lately, it was more sudden and final than most, but— *Oh Xuday – it's not finished.*

'Jecksy.' I pointed.

A group of Andros was just arriving from nowhere, mounted on these eight-legged horans they have.

'The beasts are heavy-set and strong; not fast.' Randy Driver had said, first time we saw them, coming alongside the bus. 'While the Andros riding 'em are skinny, wiry and also not fast.'

He despised them; like he did with everybody and everything. Including me, once he'd trapped me with something in my hoosh, smokes and promises that first night.

Didn't do him any good in the long run – he was already dead at the controls when our visitors arrived. He hadn't been, ten mins earlier. He was stuck by his legs and couldn't get free so I helped him, the lecherous raping, shiker. Slitting his belly wide open when I pretended to be going to slice the seat strapping. That was a help for him, actually; I wouldn't have done it if I'd known our visitors did such screamingly-agonising things so much more painfully. Good riddance – he shouldn't have driven so near the edge, showing off. And he shouldn't have done that to me the first night, either.

He was my fourth.

Er, that's my fourth *ever,* by the way – not just on this trek. It's not a habit. Or does four count as a habit? And, if we're on confessions time, I wasn't exactly a volunteer for this: it was here or the Definitely-Guilty so-called trial for castrating the two Shoikers who'd raped me. Like I make a habit of being belted round the head, tied up and raped for three days. They were lucky. I only cut their bits off; it was their own fault they bled to death. I like to think of it that way, anyway. I like to think of it very much.

Me and Jecksy were trying to separate the bodies and livies; and get the living ones out, in case the carriage blew – it was smouldering somewhere. The Andros came round us, purple-tinged face-plates like scales; eyes on stalks; mouths circular and flexible. Clothed as they were, the rest of their bodies looked fairly human. And they didn't harm us. They stood around and stared and conferred. Then looted the bus, decapitated the corpses, and everyone else who was injured. 'Maybe they don't like to hear people squawking,' Jecksy said.

'Or don't like not-fit people? The ones they killed were all injured.'

'Might be their culture – with each other as well as us aliens.'

Whichever, they collected all the goods, provisions, equipment and everything else they could prise loose, set up a camp of spring-up domes and carried on ignoring us who were still alive, and not visibly injured. They had a fire, ate – our food – drove me away when I had the nerve to approach. They retired into their dome tents as the frost took on an extra-deep bite.

Slow motion dying, but close-up: we were deep-covered in frost by daybreak, huddled together as close to the smouldering engine block as we dared crawl. It was a low ice-sun, hazed over, icicles dripping off the carriage's bodywork – until they fired the cabin as they finished packing and departed, towing a low, open-back wagon.

They never even glanced at us, clutching a couple of extra coats we'd looted from the wreckage, and we watched them depart down the slight valley slope, bouncing over the rock and gravel out-strew from our landslip. Looking around, a mite lonely-feeling, there was the near-cliff face behind us; and the narrowing, rising valley to the right. Across the rocky stream, the far side rose steeply in a near-cliff like our own.

'We follow them,' I told Jecksy. 'The only way. We need to get lower – too cold at this altitude. Nobody's going to come looking for us.' Sure, he argued, but he followed me.

It was shoik-near dusk when we caught up with them, about the time they reached their village. Big dome, and a cluster of rectangles in a complex area of single-storey erections. Jecksy was all for trying to find a way round and carry on downhill.

'Maybe not,' I said, 'they have closer food and warmth than a barren valley has. We need to take the chance and see what we can scrounge here. At least to scavenge, find a warm corner; anything to survive another freezing night.'

Of course, we were spotted sheltering in a bin, eating over-cooked dough-porg we'd scavvied. I froze, dropped the meat, and showed my hands. I always do that when I'm caught. Not so with Jecksy. Silly Shoiker kept hold of his dollop and ran. He was brought down with a kind of heavyweight bolt-arrow.

I stayed and listened while they tortured him, sliced and chopped him. Probably had this thing about finishing off the injured. He screamed an awful lot. I think the torturers were the females, but maybe not. The pieces they threw away were Jecksy. Looked like my friend Maxtan, from the block where we lived, when the glass tower collapsed the wrong way.

So what do I do here? Nothing's changed. Still the same need. I got to have shelter and food. Failing that – I attack them? Get injured, and finished off?

Oh, no. Not me. Survive the night, Girl. Whatever it takes. Whatever.

They have males and females. They look vaguely hominid. They're into sex – what they did to Jecksy. Maybe that's my angle? Find a male I can hook with? One who could use a slave, whore, pet... whatever? Not like I an't been a beddie before – couple of times, or so – Jecksy and Randy Driver, although Soldeen wasn't by choice. And Jecksy was convenient.

Okay – I scanned the males – a few in shiny leather outfits with silver-brass chest decoration. Bosses. The ones with power and influence. They could push their eyes out on long, erect stalks – weird. And they had hands with flexiclaw-fingers. Couple of them had head crests, though they might have been on a cap. There were more who were loud, and bossing others round, might have been joking... There were plenty of females among them. *Avoid them, Girl – no sympathy from there. The males, then. Try one – for whatever he might want.*

The first one whose door I knelt at threw something at me. Not food. The females were getting up. I scuttled off swiftly.

Second one the same.

The third one let me in. It was warm and light – perma-gaz fire and glowballs. There was a group, talking in Andron – clicking with howly bits, mostly. Totally incomprehensible – like their facial expressions. The one who let me in grabbed my arm and pulled. I didn't shrink or shriek. If this's it...

It wasn't murder he had in mind, but it was rape. I was half-stripped, clothes torn. Pushed down and forced forward on hands and knees. Females and kids watching – looked like laughing. Me shrieking in silence while he got down behind me, and did it to me. *Got to let him got to let him got to... Survive the night, Girl. Survive the night.*

So brutal. I seen raggerds kill each other with less intensity, back on Marrthune. Like he hated me – or humans generally. Or perhaps it's how they do it?

But I was still inside the warmth. *Is it worth it?* Looking at my massed bruises and very sore parts – I was mauled and mangled. Worth it? Yes, for a night in the warmth, with a good chance of food—

He was at me again. Behind. Just as savage and I couldn't stop myself from yelping and gasping. And he picked me up and hurled me out, nearly naked. In the frigid air outside again.

So no, it wasn't worth it. Not with some basto of an Andron with a nasty attitude to passing-through humans.

Not dead, though, am I? Like Jecksy.

Some others nearby had heard the commotion – all their mouths going OoOoOo open and shut. Must have been laughing. Eye stalks erect. Wanting to do the same?

Yeah, I reckoned they were... So they were another possible opportunity – and risk. *Look more cautiously this time, Girl.* Several threw things. Some of it was food. I scrabbled after it – ignoring their amusement – little enough cost for food, crawling and grabbing pieces of doughy bread-meat. I ate. And shivered. A few looked and laughed longer than others. Gagging, and so-near crying, I studied them between chews and trying to cover myself slightly. Not easy in shredded rags. Loud and bossy, this lot; arrogant. Didn't look likely to be any less vile than the previous raping shiker.

So... Others? A scattered lower-looking group. Less fancy garb, worn light-tan leather with no metalwork decoration. Eye stalks a bit droopy and moany little mouths. Prepossessing wasn't a word that came to mind, but beggars don't get to choose too much. So I stared back while they muttered and looked my way. *Probably deciding on their rape-pack strategy. Then what? Sliced and diced like Jecksy? Probably wouldn't survive if they all went at me the same as Bossy Basto.*

The females? A few looked into my wretched corner with silent thoughts and blank-faced stares, face-scales pale purple. They wandered off, all seeming to join up with a male. So trying to join them didn't seem too bright a prospect. Suicidal, in fact.

Back to the other male contingent, then. *Is there one I could pick? Which one's the least unpromising?* Couple of them seemed to glance my way more often than the rest. *Interested in me? Better decide, Girl. Too cold to stay out here much longer. The next one, then...*

There. He was a bit different. Taller than most, greenish hue as well as the purply tinge. Definitely interested – I delude myself sometimes, but shoik, it was cold. I was shuddering inside. I pulled the remains of my top open and stared at him. He looked away. Then back.

Yes – interested. I nodded to him – hoping he understood nods.

He didn't turn away. I opened again. *Come on, I can't be much clearer.* He glanced round the rest of the pack, deciding. Another one beat him to it. Striding over suddenly, towering over me so tall – similar to the other one – same sort of size as a human male. *As long as they don't decide to go into a partnership over me.*

Staring at me, he undid a waist stud and pulled a front panel down. *Oh Shoiks – a penis. Obviously.* Knobbly, and green-tinged. He said something and motioned to it. *Xuday – if this goes wrong...* I reached and held it, felt it, didn't dare look up for approval. It was rising, straightening. I determinedly plied at it – like with Jecksy and that basto driver Soldeen. I knew about this, of course, but wasn't exactly experienced at it.

He barked something. Pulled my head. I knew. Hadn't done this before. Mouth open, and took it in. Shoik – it was going green, and bigger, and he jerked it at my head. Felt other hands coming on me – mauling. Fruggit to Xuday – pack-rape, huh? Heard their pseudo voice-clicks and barks and howl noises. He jerked, and barked, loud. I glanced, mouth full. He drove them off – *Doogit!* His tongue lashed out at least a couple of arms' lengths, spiking a pair of the others.

They dropped away, mouths oOoO-ing, and eye-stalks wavering at him – or me – I was too preoccupied to see.

Shikes. He stopped, pulled me away, staring down. 'Koi. Ya tushishon.' And pulled my hair, up on my feet, and away... to one of the buildings – a dingy-looking one. But warm inside. Like a communal dorm with beds and screens and lockers. *A mass bachelor pad?*

At least I stand more chance in the warmth in here than the freezing temperatures outside. He dragged me to a bed near the middle; pulled screens round it when some others came in. He sat on the bed and motioned me down again. Oh Shoiks – I was really sinking, but my choices weren't great, and I sank down and opened up.

He was almost unmoving – I thought he'd do something – like I said, I've got no real history with this, so I didn't know. Felt and looked about like Jecksy's – but bright green. Hoping he couldn't do a whip-lash with it, like his tongue. *Doogit! Is this what it'll take to survive? Be better off dead. No – not if the going was like Jecksy went – and some of the other injured ones in the carriage, too. I'm the last survivor out the whole train of us – so much for a Resettlement Colony, huh?*

He was ramming my head back and forward; Shoik I was choking and panicking and he was mauling down my front. *Survive the night, Girl. Your only chance.*

It tasted spicy, like a sauce. Vile. *I usually like spice.* Tried to smile when he pulled my head up. *Still alive.*

'Yuk tu yah.' He pointed to a sink against the wall, and went to wash himself – still protruding, and practically fluorescent green – like a kid's magiwand. At least it hadn't suddenly erupted in a barbed whip like his tongue.

Stripped off, he looked vaguely hominid – same number and position of everything. *Don't think we're cross-fertile. Won't get pregnant if this goes further – if I survive that long.*

I washed, naked, but within our little screened-off area. 'Toi yu teck.' Pointing to the bed. There was no dilemma to think about, just, *Yes – I should be okay for surviving the night. He surely can't keep it up all night?* I was in the bed in less than a second, forcing a smile. They don't do smiles, so that was wasted. But he was in next to me.

And warm – thank Xuday – quite rough on his arms, almost scaley in one direction. The rest of him was smooth, though. And I couldn't see the shimmery purple-green colour-play; or the near-fluorescence below. I braced and prayed to Xuday for strength – and for keeping me alive so far – and tried to relax as his hand came over me, 'Von yak von.' He murmured, and was asleep, pinning me down flat.

Didn't last, of course. Twice more. The full real thing. Then he was up and washed. 'Von yuk tu…' He had a thing about washing, and disappeared. Back in moments with some clothing – female-suited, I imagined – or slave – *maybe the whore uniform?* He tried it against me, grunted deeply, and waved for me to dress. Surprisingly soft, it almost fitted, here and there.

Not the best night of my life, but it was an unexpected bonus to have survived it. He'd taken me in, so I might last the day as well.

It was a close thing – he'd gone off somewhere, but others hadn't, and I had to fight them off – caught one with a jaw-breaking side-swipe from the water jug, declaring I was "his" – Vonn. That was about the last thing he said, so I called him that. They backed off, demonstrating what they had in mind, and lashing barbed tongues into the air. Not aiming at me, though.

One of the other dorm occupants had a female with him, and she kept looking my way, until I signed to her about food. She turned away, didn't want to know. *What am I supposed to do all day?* I tidied up. Refilled the jug, fixed a loose panel in one of the screens, cleaned the sink area and everywhere else nearby, and cracked another wandering claw-paw with the floor brush. He retreated quickly enough. Then I just sat. Shoik – a hundred days ago, I'd been in our overcrowded tenement in the district of Subunno – on Marrthune.

They'd come round for volunteers for a new colony on Droyden – except it turned out to be Andronos where they dropped us. 'Freedom, opportunities, independence and wealth. We'll teach you the skills, languages…' Sure they did – survival, farming, fishing, forestry, mining – all on memos that we were supposed to sleep-absorb every night on the flight here – five hundred light years taking seventy-eight days of exercise and decent food. A resting period after Landing. And now sixteen days trekking over the lowlands and the plateau towards our designated area. It was supposed to be eight days, but they fucked up the maps, hadn't bothered with maintenance or sufficient provisions, got lost, broke down, and were intent on screwing us any way they could. And they thought *we* were the gutter-folk.

So here I am – sole survivor of four glassite wagons, one-hundred-twenty would-be colonists, and twelve crew. There hadn't been so much as a hint about native inhabitants or vicious wildlife. All was supposed to be wondrous. *Yeah, right – I'm alive. It's up to me now. I'll start a one-girl colony, maybe.*

Two other females joined the one who was already in the bachelor pad – more like a barn. They sat together. I went over, was noticed, then ignored. I poked one, thinking it might be an equal fight if she wanted to be narky. I did the mouth-pointing thing, and one of the others waved me outside and turn right. I nodded and went exploring.

It took ten seconds to find a sort of tented awning joined on to a kitchen shed and serving area. And half the afto to get some food. When the occupants grunted and pointed, it didn't mean Come in and help yourself – it meant Get some work done first. So I clambered over the counter and made a nuisance of myself asking and trying and testing and tasting, tossing more spice in one dish, pulling yeuk faces at another.

I didn't know if they'd tolerate it, but they did, and two of them showed me what to do – washing and cleaning and chopping some roots and lumps of meat up. My efforts were, apparently, amusingly incompetent. I served two males with whatever it was somebody gave me – something called Yog oj yundle. Unless that meant Smile while you give this to the boss guy. Apart from that, some did lots of bitching, or pointing, clucking and yelling. But they did it to each other nearly as much, so I didn't take offence.

Vonn turned up. I smiled – relief that I recognised him, as much as anything. I don't know if he smiled back, or snarled, grimaced or threatened me with a damn good fucking later on. But he collected food for himself, and I signed that I was hungry. He clicked and clacked with them like a flock of chickens, and I eventually understood that I could help myself when my shift was finished around dusk.

He wandered off with a wooden, food-filled dish. I noticed later that a couple of his Bachelor Pad Buddies didn't get the same treatment as him – they were told to return at dusk. I knew a few of the relevant words by then. I wondered if he had slightly higher status than the other gutter-types... since when? Maybe because he has a female – a whore, pet, kitchen worker. Probably the latter, to get early service in the kitchen. So his bed perk gets him food perks as well, do I?

Come sundown, I amassed as much food as I dared, and went back to the BPad with it all in a basket. Vonn seemed to be amused, or bemused, whatever. I thought I'd better share it, so I knelt and put it on his lap, opened it up, and open-handed at it, praying he wouldn't be insulted, or wolf the lot down. But he grunted and bizzed something like 'Cun dupper doo,' and took a spoonful of something greasy.

We took it in turns for a while, and I was desperate for a bigger spoon. Maybe he cottoned on, because he waved me away with the basket. Even fetched a wicker chair for me.

Yekks! This is service. Yeah, but at what cost? There's got to be a downside. Always was on Marrthune. Depends how you feel about being stuffed silly by an alien homino-Andro with a brilliant green staffy, I suppose.

But I was surviving each day and night, and that was the only thing that mattered. It was weird, degrading, painful, and very frequent. And it extended to the mouthing... kneeling – that was their usual, natural way, apparently; or standing at the sink; or being on top of him like a yorrick-rider.

I did afters in the kitchen; plus a few mornings in the repairs shed or cleaning out the livestock pens – they kept pogras and cattelyas for food and skins; horans for transport; and ten-legged little dagyas for hunting – the fastest things they had. In the kitchen, they called the long skinning knives dagyas, too. Lot in common.

So I was just starting to think I was a bit safer each night. I was still taking them one at a time, though.

Just as well.

A couple of the female Andros took it into their faceted little heads to teach me a lesson about something – though they didn't say what. It was just a sudden *Doogit!* And I was face-down in a pot of stew. It was simmering, sticking and too salty. My face was burning and I couldn't gasp or breathe so I dropped and the whole lot went over me and the other two as well. They seemed to be immune to heat like that, though.

I was burn-faced, blamed for the limited choice at dinner, snapped at by the other BPad males, and cuffed by Vonn. The female who was sniggering most went down with a severe case of sitting on a carving blade the following day, when I accidentally knocked her over and helped to extract it with a couple of deft twists. And I was sent out on field work.

Some of the other BPadders were, I think, ribbing Vonn about something, probably me. They kept glancing my way. I saw him take a side-swipe at one, and give another a quick tongue lash. Then looking at me like he was wondering about what they'd said. Like was I worth my cost? Sell me? Send me to work in the mine up the north hill? Or the pogra pens? Feed me to the spigers? It was that kind of unpromising thoughts I was getting from their attitude. Didn't feel good about it.

Don't know what else I can do to keep him happy – I'm learning their talk as fast as I can, but it's so clicky and buzzing and grunty.

A few days later, I was just returned from the outfield fruit area, scorched and worn out, parched and starving – same as all the other females. And Vonn was there at the water pump. 'Hi,' I greeted him. He grabbed me by the hair and dragged me indoors – in the BPad. 'What have I done?' I'm yelling, all a-panic, and trying not to fight.

He wanted a session, with him on my wicker chair. *Shoik, I get a mouthful of green staffy instead of the horgush pie and pixie fruit I was looking forward to. Oh Yekks…*

Doogit!!! Behind me. I'm kneeling. Being dragged. Another of them, gripping hard. Vonn tight-gripping my head. One – or more – mauling in my clothing, ripping. The click-clacking was laughter. The mauling was vicious. They didn't need to— And the sharting shaggard raped me. Pogra-style – like they preferred. While I had Vonn's bright green staffy in my face.

It was vile. Painful – brutal bastos. And it was Vonn doing it to me. *They treat me like an animal – this what they were deciding the other day, is it?* So humiliating. Queuing up for me. Hands, claws all over me – nipping and scratching. Others nearby, clack-laughing – the pallid little human alien getting it, huh?

I could have collapsed in wailing horror when they'd done; and I wanted to. But I stood, unsteady. Vonn's eyes out on stalks like sticks. I hated every one of them. Especially Vonn. *How could you? Why, for Shoik's sake? Sitting there – in my chair. Smug? Triumphant? Back with the in-crowd? Won a bet? Paid a debt?*

'This going to keep happening, Vonn?' I demanded, and stared at him – so disappointed. 'Just like the others, huh? You bastaro.'

He didn't understand a word; but he understood every syllable. One of the others was coming closer, behind me. Expecting his turn. *I fight him? Accept him. Another? How many more? Vonn stood up and someone took his place on my wicker chair. A fresh one at each end? You Shoikers – you yekking planned all this. Vonn – how could ya?*

I looked round them – all taller and stronger than me. This is how it's going to be, is it? Grinning, I think, when their face-facets ruffle like that. One grabbed. Hard, digging in, forcing me down. I glimpsed Vonn. 'You bastaro,' I snarled at him.

He got that, too. Looked away. Stepped back – washing his paws of the event.

I was down, gripped so hard I couldn't struggle with any effect. Green staffy thrusting into view. Jerking and mauling behind me. I lunged. Bit. Hard. Tore aside, spitting out. *They'll kill me.*

He roared. Clouted me. The other one was over me. I turned. Grabbed – one eye stalk. And wrenched. *Doogit!* – did he roar.

The two of them were too pained and shriek-bizzering to do much else. The others were divided in their attention – some for the two casualties, and others for stomping me down. I got a tongue lash – barbed – right across my back. I was in for it. Waited. Hurting like Shoik.

Vonn was there. Saw him stand close. Tongue slashed down – ripped my side and arm. Again across my shoulders. Shoiking hurt so much.

I waited. Long time. Pinned down by booted feet. They'll be plotting the slice-up routine. Do a Jecksy on me. Alien shuggers.

Flat down, I saw Vonn leave – open invitation for the others to do what they wanted. They didn't want to do anything. I just lay there. Could hear them, yicking and snigging. Sounded urgent; some laughing, too. Someone took hold of me, hauled me across the planking. And out the building.

I was dumped in the yard. I lay there, trying not to sob. *Survive, Girl. Survive the night.* Gradually deep-freezing, till I could move enough to crawl round the ground for my ripped-off rags they'd tossed after me. There would probably have been my other possessions, too. But I didn't have any. The rags – so easily put on; so little they covered; no use for warming, either; and so easily ripped off. I hated it, along with everyone and everything else there. And I left.

The ground was frozen already. I got as far as the barn on the far side of the livestock meadows. I'd be warmer and safer in with the pogras and cattelyas than with Vonn and his BPad cronies. Only just made it, just enough soft light from the rising Galaxia.

Shoik, I was shuddering with the cold by the time I forced in among the pogras, telling them I had more in common with them than they realised, 'So make room, you fat Yikers.'

Bad night, yeah, but I survived. 'The only thing that matters,' my Uncle Frayde once told me. 'Is that you survive. All else is irrelevant. Just survive the night.' That was the first time I'd heard that creed. Under circumstances like they were back then, with Uncle Frayde, trapped in the Goy-swamp – where my vile brothers had led us astray. And we were up to our waists in the filth, and sinking slow into the mud. He was justifying himself, Uncle Frayde. Taking hold of me and trying to climb over me to reach a branch. Justifying pushing me under to give him the leverage to reach.

He wasn't counting on me being stronger than him – I had hold of his wrists as he grabbed at me, and I forced him down. His face went under, slowly, letting bubbles out as he sank. I still couldn't reach the branch. But he made a more stable platform for me to stand on as he sank slowly overnight, and I kept above the surface till daybreak, when the searchers found me. And I didn't tell them about Uncle Frayde.

I never forgot what he'd said, either. 'Survive the Night. Whatever the cost.' I guess I owe him a lot.

Well, this is one more night I lived through. Make some tie-on footwear – thicker the better – out of cattleya leather. Got to get to lower ground, down the valley, where the nights aren't as cold. Out the plateau region.

Collect some of the root-foods and fruit from the pogra feed racks, and get moving. Stumbling mostly – hurting all over my back and sides from the tongue-lashes, and weak from lack of food and drink. *Vonn – Why did you do it? I hate you. I am so disappointed in you. I thought we had some degree of... what? Trust? Respect? Apparently not. Treating me worse than I'd deal with a body louse. What does it say about me?*

Down the valley, slow staggering, I managed to keep going all day, heading out their territory. Through lower meadows and copses... a rocky, tumbled area. I couldn't make it any further today; my feet were bleeding – the leather foot covers worn through.

I heard the dagyas coming – they make a high keening sound when they're on the scent. Trained to terrify their prey.

I'm gonna be torn apart by dagyas, much like Jecksy got from the Andro's knives, I suppose. Really weird how fatalistic you can get when your wick's down to zill.

I ran. Fell, staggered and rolled and battered myself on the rocks, and was surrounded by the pack of ten-leggers, baying and snapping. 'Come on, you vicious shikers – Get me. I don't care.' Vonn's not letting his slave whore go free, then? Wants to exact every morsel of revenge, huh? Revenge for not submitting to his capricious mood? His raping pad-mates? Whatever I'd done, yet again, he didn't like.

Vonn came, calling the dagyas back. High on his horan, black-silhouetted against the low red sun.

'I'm not taking more of that, you bastaro.'

Rigid-faced, he motioned me to stand. 'No chance in a bucket,' I told him. He gets the meaning, not the actual words, and was down off the horan, tether round my neck. I'm biting at him, clawing, and being dragged from among the rocks.

It tore my rags, and my skin, and flesh. He tied me to the saddle and I was cursed if I'd take a step. So it was a long drag through the gravel and thistle grass before he realised, or before he decided he cared. He stopped and came back. Was silent when all I did was stare at him.

He sat, drank and ate. Didn't offer me anything. I wouldn't have accepted. I stood, and turned, staggered four steps in the opposite direction – *Doogit!* – forgot the neck rope. Sank, and stayed down while Vonn clattered about with a machete, cords and dry branches, rigging up a sled to drag behind the horan – they sometimes brought dead livestock or hunting prey back on such things. One for me, huh?

Pulling my hair, he dragged me to his rig-up sled. Too confident. I lashed, got an eye stalk. Good grip. Paused before ripping sideways. I had him. Waited... I couldn't do it. Not to Vonn. I let go.

Viciously, he had my wrists bound, and strapped me down without a word, click or grunt. Facet-face flat, expressionless as always – exactly the same rope and knot pattern as they use for pogras.

'You fool. Why tie my hands? You're scared I'd have another go at blinding you? You don't even realise I just let you off the hook, do you?' Not one word would he understand. But something of the derision in my tone, maybe. 'Don't take me back. Just go fuck one the dagyas or the pogras – not me.'

His hand was pushing in the remains of my clothing. Mauled me. Hurt me. Very deliberately. He knew it hurt. Damned if I'd squeal. Couldn't breathe as I tensed so tight.

He stopped. Was on the horan and heeling it to move. Jerking away, over the rough ground. Jolted a thousand times; rolled onto my face twice. Took his time noticing.

Stopped late, dark already – the nightmare of helplessness done.

Or not.

No drink. No food. No cleaning my rips and lashes. I was so disappointed in him. He could have—

He undid the straps, hoisted me up and draped me over a fallen tree trunk. He was savage. Again. Bare-arsed to the whole damn plateau and planet. How could he? I'd really thought—

Staring at a rock coyer with huge teeth, I took it. No choice.

And was left there, neck tethered again, while he rolled in a snug sheffler blanket. Want me to freeze to death, do you? No way. I don't give up. The dagyas were huddled together. I crawled among them. Smelled better than the pogras, but less welcoming. Snapping. Till I straight-fingered one's eyes out. It whimpered. The others let me in.

Come morning – which was something of a surprise in itself – I was ordered up. Wouldn't. Couldn't – too stiff and weak and dry. Even for another lashing with his tongue-barb. *Doogit! – he knows how to use that.* It was agony. Deeper. I manged to stand. Go on then. Flay me. I was naked. He could easy do it. Tongue flickered. Yuhh! Speared me. Left side. Below the ribs. Tore out, barbs ripping. Dragging me off my scarcely-functioning legs. Onto my knees. Don't know what I was supposed to learn from that. I just looked at him, trying to understand as well as hate.

He was on me, slapping my face – that was temper. Too hard. Not chastising or teaching. *Just temper, you basto.*

I think that was the first time I ever truly regretted surviving the night. And I carried on regretting it just as much when I was strapped and bound on the drag-sled again. The dagyas snarled round their victim. Shoik off. Except my mouth was too dry to say it. What? Two... three days since I saw water? Same for food. Or shelter from the sun.

The day was beyond nightmare. Taking me back for what? Vengeance at the claws of the de-staffied one? The half-eyed one. I'm going to be flayed? Do a Jecksy on me? Shoik, I still hear his screams. Gonna make me an example to the others – the females? They already know better than to do whatever I did wrong – whatever I did to deserve my face in the stew, or sold out to a queue of Vonn's cronies.

Can't defy him if I'm strapped down over a log for any of them's entertainment any time. Mince me up for pogra food? Live prey for the dagyas? Whatever.

They can hardly starve me – I couldn't eat now anyway. *Be dead soon. Desiccated. Can smell something festering. Arm. Or back?*

So much for a new life on a new planet... resettlement opportunity... Saw the sun. Stared at it. Scorching my eyes out. Didn't hurt any more than everywhere else.

The sled had stopped. He was there. Couldn't see him. Putting water to my mouth. Couldn't drink it. Wouldn't. Lips cracked solid. He was dribbling water into my mouth. *Y' too late, Vonn. Three days too late.* 'Fuck off, Vonn.' No point in me surviving purely for your entertainment.

He was unstrapping the bindings. Long hesitation before he untied my wrists. Fingers dead anyway. Gone white.

He was kuku-ing – lots of little kuku sounds. Xuday-alone knows what they meant, but he was doing it all the time the water was dribbling over me. Couldn't open my mouth anyway. Or swallow.

'Keert,' he said. That's a plea.

Softening, are you? Huh – too late. Should'a done that when y'ignored my head being stuffed in the stew; before y' shared me round; when I didn't rip your eye off. *Y' just too thick to realise any of it.*

'Keert, mi tiako.' He's called me that in bed sometimes. Tiako. I'd taken it as the first sign of endearment from him. Fat-boy's chance.

But... maybe he's stopped digging? Giving each other one more chance?

I tried to drink. Really couldn't. Couldn't hold the flask. He splashed my face. Xuday, it stung. Choked, coughed – too dry to cough right.

He kept it up, dribbling water in my mouth and over my face... looked at some of the festering lash marks. He stared at me. If it was me doing the looking, I'd be staring at me in shame for what I'd done. But Vonn? I don't know what he was thinking. Something he dabbed on the rip in my side really stung like concentrated antiseptol. And then he was splashing it over my back and shoulders and arms and I was screaming all over. Not that he noticed.

I was sitting up, hands tingling back to life, eyes seeing more, the lashed areas calming down. We were on the edge of a field – I managed to stand, and look round – the south perimeter field where the pogras forage. A couple of dozen pogras were gathered round the water troughs close to us. Vonn went over and patted one, said something.

I went cold inside. *This is what you've brought me back to, huh? Being pogra-fucked by you and your gruesome mates? Think again.*

He climbed up on his horan, called to me and the dagyas, motioned us to follow.

He turned to check we were doing. *Not me. I'm not going back to that.* He understands nodding and head-shaking now, and there was no mistaking my refusal to go with him. 'I'm not an animal, Vonn. I don't live with'em, sleep with'em, get screwed with'em, and right now, I don't walk with'em, either. I'm a human, you alien shiker.'

I imagine he got nothing more than the refusal. He was back in my face, jabber-clicking something, pointing in the direction of the village – Ves Niche, they call it. I stepped past him, the other direction. 'I'm not one of your livestock.'

Unconvinced, he snapped, jabbered, tongue-flickered. But no way was I going back there; not to that. Him sitting up there high and mighty on his horan, and me tottering along with the pack. I tried to get past him again, holding his hand up to stop me, continuing his orders, bizzing at the dagyas – they came snarling at me, all teeth and red eyes. Didn't help.

It took some time, a leg bite and threat of a brass collar for me; and an eye-stalk in my grasp for him – he's slow on that. But we compromised, and we all walked. Vonn and me at the front with the horan on the lead, and the dagyas chasing round.

Couple of hundred steps and I was on my knees, fell against Vonn, clutched at him for support and he clamped an arm round me. I think he liked that, half-carrying me. *This'll look better... except I'm still in ripped-up rags.* So I clutched them round my chest and made a bit of a fuss about it. He glanced down. Clearly needed more than a hint, so I staggered and tried to pull them together more obviously.

He realised. Took his jacket off and draped it round my shoulders. Long enough to cover right down my thighs. I did a lot of smiling and nodding – he gets them.

There. That's better. Come on, Vonn. Learn the lesson – I'm not for public consumption.

We stumbled into the village. I stumbled, anyway. Not totally without cause – I was absolutely done in, but I could have managed better. *Just learn to be protective, Vonn. Not thoughtless, hmm?* The Boss males weren't around. The few visible Middle-Tier males didn't do more than glance our way, though the lower-group mostly watched us as we headed for the Bachelor Pad.

At the entrance, I stopped. Got to make sure. 'So where do I go?' Pointing down the side of the building where the dagya and pogra pens were. 'Or inside?'

At least he understood that; and I reckon he got the implied 'and if it's the pogra pen I'll not stop till I'm ten villages away.'

'Eck yur,' he escorted me inside. Inside, I sagged in relief. Outside, I swelled. *Thank you, Xuday.*

I sank again. Nothing was different – Why had I thought..? Back where I started.

No. This will not stay the same. Instant plan to stash some food and water, check the route past the pogra fields... be gone one night. I have lots of instant plans.

We got to the bed space. He waved to the wicker chair. Like it was mine. *You want me kneeling there? Got your shag-pack lined up? Never again. Not anywhere near it.*

As with other occasions, he didn't understand a word, but got the gist. The wicker chair went. *Yeah, maybe he could change – and me too, if I knew what they expected.* Our faltering discussion sort of agreed that the screens stayed; I'd go in his bed; nothing with watchers or extras. The pogra-style was their natural way; they all did it without thought.

'I'm not them. You got a classier girl in me.' I think he understood that, even if he didn't agree with it, but I had to make a stand on something. See if he valued me at all.

He cuddled me that first night back. Didn't attempt anything more. Maybe he did value me more – wanted an improved relationship – so I stayed still. All night.

Friends came for him in the morning. Work. I didn't know what. He was reluctant. I pushed him to go. He decided to trust me, I think.

I drank, washed, cleaned myself. Went to the kitchen and took food. Threatened the two who objected. And took more. Fitted higher screen panels round our bed. Made a straw doily of a home sprite to hang over the sink. I obtained another chair.

Vonn was unsure, but accepted it. That was my half-way offering.

It was two more nights before I cuddled back. And we did it.

I survived four more nights; one at a time. He stayed away the fifth night, and I was afraid he'd left the way clear for his usual scag-pack to come round for their fun night. I sat in my chair against the wall, all night with a fruit-cutter blade and very bad attitude. I had a drink beside me, and some leftover porg steaks to suck on. Furious that I'd so blindly trusted him.

No-one came close. Was his night out simply a jolly with friends, or with a whore? Had he changed to night shifts? A nocto hunting trip, or whatever? I didn't want to impinge on that, if it was innocentish. Just the same, I gave him the cold arse when he returned after dawn, wobbling at the knees and everywhere else that moved. He saw me sitting with the blade, and began to realise what I'd been thinking. So we talked it through, explaining and signing and agreeing, I think, on him letting me know in advance. It might be agreed between us, I'd have to see.

Eight, as I recall, more nights and days I survived, and I was working mornings in the fields and afters in the kitchen. I didn't care what they thought about me being there; and they saw it my way when Myo Yik Yik something-or-other went off with a broken wrist – twist-shatter. They're so brittle. They'll learn.

Plus, I did a couple of sessions in the pogra pens, and in the meat-processing building. The pogras have eight legs, and there's a preference scale they have regarding how each pair is prepared and cooked. They all look and taste the same to me.

My work level and an idea for organising the processing all earned me credits with the tallyman. He was a mid-level Andro who arranged all the finances for the Low Levellers like us. Vonn could do that job, I decided, with a bit of help.

Tallyman had me on the beads; same rate as the others – females and males. My credits were doing okay. I got him to link it under Vonn's name. More than a togetherness token – it gave Vonn total control. Might help with him. And I still had my flight plan in place. In case. Mostly by way of a stash of heavy-duty clothes and dried food in the pogra-pens.

That was when I decided we needed a hobby. The obvious and ideal one would be for me to learn Andron. The corollary of which was that he began to learn Stang – which would be valuable if outworld contact ever came to the community.

I was organising the meat processing shed within the half-year; and I synched production with the Low Kitchen, and then the Middle-Levellers' Kitchen, too. They provided meals to the three Boss Houses, and I had a few ideas about how to develop their choices – *fussy load of High-rackers, they are.* I wasn't fluent in Andron, but I was okay, making myself understood in Low-talk and Mid-High. Need to work on the High tones and phraseology more. Vonn is doing pretty well at Stang, though he skips out with his mates sometimes when we're supposed to be learning. That's okay. He's actually not Vonn – he's Ssssprrr-ijing-jirrip to his mates, so I stick with Vonn, and told him it's a word in my own dialect of Marrthune, meaning Lord. 'We used to call the head of our district Vonn, in homage.' I told him. 'A title of respect.'

He likes it. He calls me Tikin. So do the others. I thought it was a similar sort of name as Vonn, but he confessed it was the name of a fictional children's character in their storybooks. I found one of the books when I visited the communal domes where All-Class families met, could eat, exercise, let children play, read… I found Tikin, and managed to read the stories of an awkward little outsider, coloured red-blue – which is a disliked combination, especially when it's sparkling and glittery – and she was a sneaky, bossy, fidgety and despised little thief who they couldn't get rid of.

I sat there in the rec room with some of the other females and their progeny. I was empty. The butt of fun. That kinda crushed me. *So that's what they really think of me.*

I didn't bother with anything much in the following days. Tolerated Vonn's attentions. Left the others to it.

Cried, actually, when it sank in, thinking about it. *I'm not like that. I'm not. And if that's what they're thinking...* I checked my stash. Added some extra clothes. *Tomorrow night, when he's out with his mates.*

I was tackled about my sudden change of attitude and non-work ethic by Vonn. He was curdled with me, he said, thinking I was being my usual unknowable alien self. *We're heading back to Square One at descent speed.* I couldn't bring myself to tell him how utterly disappointed I felt – betrayed. So I handed him the book, open at the most me-hating page that I loathed.

He looked. And read. And turned pages. And looked at me.

I thought he was going to toss it on the bed, like he usually does, and dismiss me with his left-hand wave. He didn't. He took my hand and sort of nuzzled it against his cheek – never done that before – and left.

Didn't return that night – I would have gone then if I'd known he'd be out all that night. *Brought his mates' night forward, has he? An extra Cackle-at-the-Tikin-Whore night is it?*

Alone all night. *Yet again. I need to be gone. I work like shike. Give him total access to it all. No appreciation. Despises me. I'm not sitting here again feeling sorry for myself. Next night he's out, I'm off. I'll work till then – they can think I've gotten over it.*

He was back around noon, when I was coming off the roots field with an electro wagon full of trimmed Kyicks for sale to the up-valley neighbouring community. He took hold of me. 'Kitchen,' I said, and tried to pull free. 'Afternoon in the kitchen.' But he kept his grip and insisted I go back to the BPad with him.

Our bed wasn't there. *Going to chuck me out with it? Good.* But it had been moved, to one of the separate rooms on the end of the dorm hall. And he was saying about yichy... yichy... That was the individual homes outside, where the couples and families lived.

He never called me Tikin again. Nor did anyone else.

The separate room was so much better. Better than being dead up the mountain in a burning carriage, anyway. And better than being publicly hanged for killing the two raping shoikers back on Marrthune.

Then we talked with the Tallyman, and we had permission, and enough credits, to have a cabin like the Mid-levellers have. And Vonn got a new jacket – the darker, smarter leather like the Middlers have.

'Jivbwij huiq hehjs,' he explained, 'Promotion.' He was shift manager at the mine, although it wasn't only a mine, it did small-scale smelting, as well, and fashioning into small mechano parts for machines, and some items for decoration.

The seasonal dagya hunt for mountain shogats went very well, with nearly all the village taking part. We even caught enough to sell some meat to the other villages; and I said we could take some live ones back and keep them for a time. We processed more meat than ever before. Not that anyone told me – I overheard two of the females saying it. I know they still think of me as Tikin, but they don't say it to my face. Not after what happened to Glil Kiv Nicun's mouth. They definitely suspect me of that one.

They're right.

They think I'm more of a smart pet that's been trained, like a salunkey. There was a salunkey at the fair that passed through, up from the Ovalar Plains. That was good – they sold all sorts of things on their travel market, and bought our stuff, too.

One of the Plains Andros at the fair was telling me he'd seen humans like me about twenty days travel down the main valley. 'Just three of them in a cabin that's like a little fair that stays in one place... for buying and selling all kinds of goods from places all over the plateau and plains.'

He said there had been a ship in orbit for several days, and more humans had come down, but he didn't know where they'd gone.

I suppose the base where we'd landed is still there. Maybe they'd been out to search for us, probably more for the four vehicles than we would-be colonists. Maybe they were glad to be rid of us – useless drivers and maintenance men who got lost whilst driving cranky old bus carriages like idiots without being sufficiently provisioned – plus unlucky with the particularly early onset of the Alto winds that froze the plateau solid in winter. The landslide, insects and all the rest didn't help, either. We were just fated.

Right back then, when the Andros villagers had found our wrecked carriage, they were out on a foraging trip, and had seen us rolling down the cliff-face. And came to see. It's their custom to kill off the injured, and take whatever is left of any value. No judgement call – it's simply how they are. 'They were foraging, so they foraged,' Vonn told me. He hadn't been there, but it was what they did.

There were no other humans settled in that area back then. Nearly a year ago, is it now? The villagers had seen a few in the plains on trading trips, passing through, surveying, lost, whatever. But I was the only one who'd ever been in The Valley. Xorichi, they call us humans; I don't think it's derogatory.

That travelling fair, though... Flutes! It was so good – a revelation. They were heading up for the higher valley communities and onto the plateau for the high season. They had goods from the lowlands, the plains, the lower valleys communities; and wanted some things we had – the machined parts and the high-value metals. The salt-smoked riverlings... the silver decorations and gifts.

But most – the evenings – the rides, the lighting, music, games, even the community fire. OmiXuday! They were dancing... and singing!

Both a revelation – I didn't know they did either, Me and Vonn danced. Like something slow and close together and I was so clumsy and nearly falling and tripping and lost in what to do next. Vonn knew, of course, and he had the suppleness and leg-length to do it. I felt so shown-up, but there was this mass of clicking when the dance was over and we were included in the congratulations... and singing... I knew a lot of the words – but not how they went into songs. You wouldn't believe how folk distort words to fit into melodies – completely unrecognisable. And the tunes... cadences... so ethereal. Like it was a different species again that was doing the singing... and the music, the instruments. It was just magical, the whole evening, together. For all that I'd shown myself up with the failures at dancing and singing, the Andros seemed to take to me more and I felt, like, more like I was part of them.

And Vonn – different again from his serious village self. Maybe he gets lively with his mates on his night out, but I've never seen him carefree like that before and I hugged him and he squeezed me back and muttered – something.

I got drunk… I didn't know they had booze – I never used it on Marrthune. Saw too many and what it did to'em. They were passing the flasks round in the after-singing flop-about, and I just thought it was some tradition and joined in. Didn't know what it was till it hit me, and I was laughing at the jokes, and told'em things about the tenement, and when I tossed a thief off the balcony – I never confessed that before – he lived, just, so I don't count him on my kematian tally.

They had this game where we all had to tell about something embarrassing that happened to us and I said my worst, about my brothers catching me playing with myself and the handle of the suction grinder in the kitchen. But the Andros seemed to think it was fairly normal, judging by the non-reaction – polite so-called laughter and funny looks.

And we had to tell truths – and Vonn said… The bastard said he loved me. The bastard. How could he do that to me? For my truth I said I was glad I killed my brothers but I missed my sisters. But Vonn said it had to be about now and I said I felt trapped. And they thought I meant in Ves Niche, but I didn't, I meant trapped by the game and I couldn't say and they said I had to and I said it made me realise I… had feelings for… Fuckit, I loved him too.

He sort of cuddled me all the way back to our cabin. And that was my worst-best night in Ves Niche. We kind of talked about it, and understood, and we couldn't open up too much. But we know, anyway now, and it don't need saying lots.

Vonn's been taking me out, just the two of us, to the communal recreation areas which don't sound great but have bars and diners and rec rooms for grownies and children and a library. And we started going to the nearest one and sometimes went to the other one instead.

It seemed like I was more accepted after that.

They were saying that winter was late this year. So I must have been here well more than a year. The frosting covered the high slopes on both sides of the valley, and it didn't melt off in the daytimes. 'It's late, but it's come hard,' Vonn said. 'Nobody goes up there much, especially in winter.'

'I see the highland wildlife comes down in numbers, though.'

'When the hyungers come down they raid our livestock. They're patient hunters, lie in wait with rows of teeth on display. Once they get a grip, there's no making them release you.'

'They edible? Might be worth trapping some?' I wondered.

'Tough meat.'

'We could try slow-cooking – like in the ground pits – it might tenderise the meat.'

So one of the others organised hunting events, and I tried some different methods and cuts and had a meat-evening out in the yard with a small amount of the spiurt-beer – I wasn't going near any more truth and red-face games again.

'I'm glad you're with us,' Chi Kin said. He's the tallyman. His two ladies nodded – their version of nodded, anyway. 'You've been good for Ves Niche. Brought more life here.'

There was quite a bit of snow up the higher slopes, too, which Vonn said was unusual. And it drifted and settled and blew over the plateau edges forming huge overhanging cornices that built up and up until they collapsed in great white avalanches down into the valley. And the snow began to accumulate in the higher parts of the valley, too, so we brought the cattleya in and had them indoors and in the big barns and communal places, people and livestock living together. A warm, rich atmosphere it made, too.

'You always lived like this? Where you came from?'

I could so have taken offence, and I didn't know if they were serious or joking, but I decided they weren't being nasty about it, and let it go.

'Good job we got all that spare meat... and the hyugars.' They looked my way, but they aren't the compliment-giving kind.

But we all survived the winter and learned so much about each other, especially me and Vonn. More than I preferred – they do these truth games too often, like being stuck in Halsinge Terminal all winter with your nosy granny.

It's a really strange kind of relationship we have – I always defer to Vonn nowadays: he's the jealous, unstable type; gets possessive. We're a Rock together.

I could grab an eye stalk faster than he could react, but I could never stop that barbed tongue. It's called the basis of mutual respect.

It really is strange – the other Andros don't understand it. Love isn't something they do. The concept is beyond them. For Vonn to have said that, not so long ago – I knew then it was special.

We're pretty free with the sex. As long as it's only the two of us, there's nothing barred.

I'm thinking maybe I'm with seed – there's something in here. Interbreeding isn't known of – any kind of relationships previously unknown. So we're going to wait and see.

Certainly has the village agog – this lot sure know how to put on their agog faces.

We're both pretty content with our higher status. Both Middlers now – and high-rank ones at that. It's not like we could ever become Top Tier Andros; they're born, aristocrats. But it's possible to be, like, a top man among the Middlers. They're the ones who run things, not the Bossmen. They're the ancient titled ones with ownership of the valley, but they don't interfere with the smooth running of what happens in it.

I see futures here. Even now, as I see opportunities where and when I might leave. But I'm not leaving here; I'm actually appreciated. These Andros see what I am, what I can do. They know I'm bright and quick, and have greater, wider knowledge than they do, and yet, I always give the credit to Vonn – he needs it; he deserves it. We share it in our own way – certainly not like any other couple in Ves Niche.

I expect that's why we're in the High Four of the Council now.

Yes… no way am I going back to human society, not with my history – I was offered this colony choice as the alternative to being hanged in public after I killed the two men who raped me for three days back at Tenement, on Marrthune. And certainly not recently, since Vonn and I learned to understand each other more, and how much we could mean to each other.

Humans were seen in the valley, heading slowly this way. 'They seem to be exploring, merely looking at plants and animals and rocks; studying them, taking samples, specimens... and many pictures and measurements.

With an Andros guide, they eventually arrived in Ves Niche. Some of the High-Middles and the Bossmen met them and talked with them – they sent for me as well, mostly as translator, although I didn't let it rest at that for long.

One of the human visitors came to me afterwards. 'You're so valued here – the rep... How'd you get here? Where are you from?'

I wouldn't say anything about myself, but he was looking at me, like he suspected things. But he didn't actually know, or suspect very specifically, where I was from. He couldn't know about the prison ship that had dropped us here, or the convoy over the plateau. No reason to know about any of my history. So why should I endarken him?

Next time a party of humans came up the valley, the following Spring, they knew about us, and me. Asked to speak through me again, as translator. Even gave me a Nomina title – In Between, like it was my name. I guess they didn't know about the bar on Marrthune of the same name – between the Tenement and The Tower of Saffej.

It was all talk about what the Andros mined – what minerals, what they farmed in crops and livestock – more with a view to trading than taking it up themselves.

'But that's always an option.' The tall man who seemed to be the Second or Third status-wise was trying to nudge a little warning our way.

'Not on our land,' the Andros were adamant about that. I reinforced their message with a few accounts of how they traditionally despatched those who upset them – like Jecksy.

Tall Guy was thinking about that, as a counter-argument to them trying to move in on Andros land.

'You want a trading cabin?' I said. 'Try a couple of hours' trek south of here; there's a cross-tracks between long-valley travellers, and anyone coming down from the plateau either side. That's unclaimed land; you could create a safe passageway and meeting centre. Overnighting; buy, sell and bargain for trade.'

Talk about riddled with suspicion, as the song goes on Marrthune – 'Oh, yes, if it's that promising, how come you're not doing it?

'The Andros are farmer-miners, not traders. They wouldn't entertain the idea of setting it up themselves when I proposed it before the winter. Besides, they could always descend on you one dark night, and... er, take over.'

They looked a mite dubious at that prospect.

'But they won't.' *They might descend on you, but they wouldn't take up trading – it's not in them.* 'You'll be fine down there.'

'Er... maybe we started a bit on the heavy side? I'm Donnal Faredeel, from Dojdi.'

That summed him up. 'Come on – you're either a fair deal, or you're dodgy. Which is it?'

So he was on the back foot, and changing the subject, 'You're from Marrthune, aren't you? From your accent—'

'From checking up on me, more like. I bet you looked up some of the news from Marrthune, didn't you?'

He looked a touch caught-out, 'Well, there's—'

'Sorry, you wasted your time. There's nothing I want to know, recall or relive. I'm well away from there.'

'I looked you up on Gargoyle – You're Karim Karmir – you changed your name.' He had a smirk, like he thought he knew things about me... maybe to hold over me.

You know about the bollock-deprived Ravi and Sher, do you? The pair whose families swore to get me for their gelding? And bleeding out? You going to threaten to reveal my whereabouts to them? Or does Karmir mean something disgusting in Dojdi?

'Your file – Prison... two convictions for murder.'

'In absentia – they didn't hold the trial. And it's not up to date. I've bagged five now. You could be six—'

'Yeah well —'

I had him by the throat, 'I'm contented here, so, one more word on the subject of my past, and you're definitely six.'

'Contented? Here?'

Death-defying derision comes so mindlessly to idiots, does it not? 'Yes,' I told him, 'More than I've ever been. I never had happy times on Marrthune, so contented is pretty good.'

He was a brave little chappie, give him that. He was back later, with my deep file. Two sheets of semi-trans plazpap. My old file from Marrthune.

It was all there, the front page displaying all the statistics. Not realising he was counting down his own death list, my smirking visitor began to read them aloud.

'IQ 192/188

'Functional coordinates of somatotyping 53 / 17 / 4 / 11...' the digits continued, meaning nothing to me. But he sneered up and down me as he quoted my body-type classifications, as though agreeing or disagreeing with some long-forgotten doctor's measurements. I remember that doc – so lucky to still be breathing after my physical, with that caryoscope lodged in his throat; lecherous BS.

'Aptitude 7x7... Adaptability P8... Social quotient F-8.6' Dodgy Don looked at me again, big smile. *It could well be your last; make the most of it.* 'Sociable kind of girl, huh?'

He mumbled his way through my soma-graphs and analyses – my latent willpower, strength in mentality, determination quotient. Went on to Blood type – DNA – DoB – Planet of origin...

Impatient, I pulled it from his grasp. The data continued down the page... all the *me* data – what I am, what I am like... Some collective view of me.

I turned to the next page – a picture of me as an urchin; another, at the prison. A third – stylo-rigged – I never, ever looked *that* whorelike.

My record... my family... my crimes... punishments. Not much of what had happened to me – why I'd done it... my family and what shykers they had all been. That dump of a tenement.

My physical measurements – height, weight, BMI, bust, waist, hip, ILM, reach…

Gyrick rating…

Racial Ex 9/9/00/9

'You see this file, Donnal Faredeel from Dojdi?' I waved it at him. The front page is what I am. It is what I do. What helped me to survive among the Andros. All that is what *they* see me as – how they relate to me, treat me. It's why the Andros have come to appreciate me.'

'As opposed to?' That superior smirk.

'How the humans see me, judge me.'

'What? Your crimes? Your punishments? Why you are here?'

'Partly that, perhaps. But mostly… see… there, in the top corner – my code type.' I pointed to the black digits.

'Yes – a code. Everyone has one. Mine's 3 - 9 - S. Yours is… er…' He twisted his head to see, '3 - 8 - D?'

'Yes, it's how humans think of me.'

'By your code type?'

'In a way. It's the fourth rating measurement on the Physical Attributes List.'

'Huh?'

I stood and thrust my chest out. '38D. That's the only aspect of me that *you* people see. Now shoik off before I set Vonn on you.'

WITH A WILL OF HER OWN

She was only eight with a will of her own.
I her brother, just half-grown,
Looked after her, a wilful child
Who'd chase the comets, running wild.
Our playground then was an orbiting yard
Of spacecraft junk and life was hard

Till one dark day when she slipped away
With a gang of tentacled Alversay.
Our parents said, 'It's the rod for you.'
And lashed me red and burned me blue,
As into the cellar I had to crawl.
For a week alone in a hog-beast stall

For losing sight of their precious child.
And she just stood and gently smiled.
When she sauntered back without a care
'We've all been down to the Montag fair;
It's great on the rides,' she grinned,
And laughed to see my back was skinned.

------oOo------

She reached eighteen with a mind of spite
But I had the duty of oversight.
But she cared not, and was prone to run
To any place where there might be fun
Though we still hung around the orbiting yard
And earned some cash and studied hard

And worked on wrecks for scrap and spares
Till she vanished again without a word
And I was left to explain the loss
For I was adult and responsible then
So they locked me up for six long weeks
On the prison Moon with the alien horde.

They searched and probed and yelled at me
'You've killed her off! Where is she now?'
Till back you came with face alight
And didn't care that I'd lost one eye
And broke a leg while you've been off
With a crowd of Lizards from Alga Hoff

------oOo------

At twenty-eight, with a ship of our own
We worked the planets and asteroids;
A cargo here in utmost haste
Or tourists there at leisurely pace
We stuck together for safety's sake
Till she shrugged away in a barrel roll

Deserted our group of passenger folk
Who'd paid for the sights of Calder Yoke
Away she'd gone and I was left
In an ion storm on a wintry morn
To take the blame for losing four
In the forbidden zone of Orton Tor.

She'll not have given a thought to me
For half a year. But my appeal time's up,
And I stand in a group a dozen strong
In an airlock cold. Convicted all,
And waiting now till the hour's on noon.
It's the vac we'll all be breathing soon.

THE GALAXY'S GREATEST CRIMINAL.

'What's that? On the VV's?'

'Big news, Dad. About Gonquin. That one you always go on about.'

'Not dead is he?' I upped the screen size to fill the wall – *Oooh, no. Too big – that's girl's too well-endowed to be double-size on the lounge wall.*

'Naw.' My kids were actually paying attention to the news. Must be a first for any kids anywhere on Paradijo.

'So what *is* he all over the news for?' *Shuggery – if they're making this much fuss on the VVs...* This is upsetting. I come in the room and get confronted by this. Gonquin's on the news. 'What's happened? He's not been killed in there, has he?'

Robbie called back over his shoulder, still focused on the screen, 'No, he's been released under the general All-Planet Amnesty—'

'It's part of the celebrations for the Unity of the Planets.'

Released! Gonquin? Released? Just like that? He's out?

'Don't look like that, Dad.'

'Just cause he's your hero, eh, Pops?'

'Always has been,' I mumbled, glued to the screen, ignoring my kids' joshing. *Pitfire! Kids, always nattering when you're trying to catch something vital on the vivis... Who'd have'em, eh?*

'He was a monster, Dad; robbing and killing and all sorts.' Molly was taking it a bit far, pulling the ugliest faces any little girl ever did – except Sareen H'tog, of course. Yessie and Maudie were enthusing in their agreement, 'Absolute fiend.' And they were at it, too, mock firing zip-guns round the room, focusing the really intense fire on me. *Conflict,* I thought, *it's always conflict with kids these days. It's the crud they join in with, on the vivis.*

'He's nothing of the sort. He's the saviour of the Union... practically its founder. Who do you think was most responsible for uniting the Eighteen Planets?' I sidewayed over to her, using my foot to ease her pet yurkle onto its back for tickles.

'Eh?' Paffy and Dave started going on at me. 'You shouldn't be supporting an interstellar criminal.'

'*Successful* interstellar crim,' I pointed out. 'Most successful ever.'

'Not *that* successful Dad.' They all call me Dad, though half of them know I'm their uncle – but we're all just one happy family of squabblers under the surface, as well as on top. 'He's been incarcerated in Carson PoC for the past four years.'

I ignored their plebeian sniping, flicked the yurkle over again, and sipped an orange fruity that one of them had foolishly left within my reach. 'Look at his record, Padge,' I settled back. 'Major robbery crimes on eleven of the planets that are now finally united. And why are they united? Because he was so well organised that they had to start working together to combat him – sharing info and resources.'

'They got him in the end, though—' Another mock-burst of stellar and zip-gun fire in my direction. *It's always conflict with 'em. Why can't they be peaceable, like me?*

'He's lucky to have only done four years.'

'Awe, Molly, leave him be. Done his time. United the planets, and he's free now. You sure it's not just some temporary thing?'

'Full amnesty, Dad.'

'My arnicles! It's disgraceful.' Padge's language gets worse. 'They shouldn't have included him in it. Got away with murder, he did, dooning Cunrabite—'

'Language! Maise, and No – he used paranoxide. We dev— he used an insta-vap hand weapon. Took places by total surprise; very rarely hit the same planet twice in a year, even hugely-populated ones like Broober and Salvation.'

'You sound like you're on his side, Dad?'

'Always am. You know – me and the little guy.'

'More than usual.' Maise might be a mite slack with her language, but she was perceptive with her observations. Takes after her father.

'It's true, Dad, you always root for him on the vivi Make-ups, and all you ever say is, "Well somebody's got to be on his side."' Just what I need, other daughter joining in, all condemnation and accusatory, calling him a dooning Cun— Till I pointed my warning finger, and she took the hint.

'Sure, why not? He did a lot towards unity, like I said. Inter-planet security is so good because of him; almost entirely to his credit. Plus…' Quick glance round to make sure I had someone's attention, 'the paranoxide is used on most planets now as a first-call anaesthetic – emergency packs always contain it – viable for any nerve-based species. It was Al who gave that to the Union. Free. He'd be a multi-trillionaire if he'd charged for it.'

'Dad! He'd have to go to the Union O Bank—'

'And they'd catch him.'

'But think how rich he'd be.' *Got to look on the positive side, haven't you?*

The yurkle thought about nibbling my ankle. It changed its mind when I flicked some orange gunge its way. 'In any case, he had that Drion Drive ship – eight times the speed of any other – he would have escaped – like he always does on the Make-ups.'

'You know they're not real, Dad.'

'Don't tell me that,' I feigned horror at the thought that the VV Make-ups might not be total truth. 'He'd use that cloak unit to hide his ship, and escape, invisible—'

'Dad! You're being silly on purpose! Stop it.' Bullied by nine kids. I never stand a chance against such odds. *Why do folks have'em?*

'They must be real,' I told'em. 'I heard ages ago that joint-ops troops were adopting cloak technology for their attack troops. How else would they have been so successful against the Fringe Rebellions?

'They had Gonquin's ultra-speed ship techno... operating under his cloak shielding... and using our— using Al's other big development, the paranoxide. They used it as a mass pacifier before the troops landed.'

Sheesh! Just saying it, I had to smile – the times we'd done that. Yes, the Union Forces learned a lot from our tactics, as well as our drive – *My drive.*

'They say he's being deported from GeeCee—'

'And he's coming here, to Paradijo.'

'Is he, indeed? Wonder why?' Just looking round their eager, dubious, awed, untrusting little faces... *Coming here? This is good news.* 'I wonder if he's changed much? They never show genuine pics of such folk on the vivis, do they? It infringes their privacy rights to a private future.'

'What are you saying, Dad? You remember what he looked like, in the real?'

'Did you really meet him?'

'Did you know him?'

They took my vacant shrug as a "yes".

'What? You mean, not from the old newsies?' Eager little faces, kids these days. Full of opinion and socio-propaganda off the memms and VV rads. Then the thought of your dad actually knowing the biggest, most villainous criminal in the galaxy! The wow! bit was washing all over'em.

Whenever I smiled, Harriet knew what it meant. Harriet's my eldest – well, not *my* eldest, exactly. 'You *knew* him Dad! You *really* knew him?'

So they were all clamouring round – like the glamour rubbing off because Dad might have been closely acquainted with the Union's most famous-ever criminal.

And the most successful, too. All his proceeds stayed hidden. The Union Forces never recovered anything, except from the last job where they caught him. Sheer carelessness on his part – not following the plan. But he never split on where it was stashed, or who his accomplices were, how come he'd developed a ship drive like the Drion... the cloak technology... the paranoxide... all of it.

We'd agreed: if one of us gets caught, we say nothing. The other stays silent – it's not as if talking would help our case, not the treacherous way the Govvies carry on these days. Can't trust'em to really cut your sentence for cooperating – throat, more like.

We all watched the live-time cast on the VV, and my wondrous nonad bajjered and wheedled and threatened if I didn't say how I knew him, and when and where. Course, they had no memories of back then – I'd selectively suppressed them at the time – that paranoxide has so many uses.

And yeah, it *was* profitable, successful; we had billions stashed away – all included in the amnesty, and not touched since the day. Small price for the Union to pay for my genius inventions – especially the Drion drive, which had completely revolutionised travel and communication around the Union. Enabled it, we did, me and Al; the whole federated planetary region, one way and another. Deserve every last arshin of our hoard, we do.

'Well,' I cut the kids' mob tactics short, 'you'd better get used to calling him Uncle Al in future. Or *Dad*, some of you.'

THE SECRET OF VONDUR'EYE

'Do you know what is meant by The Secret of Vondur'Eye?'

Vondur'Eye? Is that what this's about? After all these years? They're resurrecting Vondur'Eye? As if I could ever forget. But it's buried. Hidden. It has to be – You don't keep anything like that uppermost. As if there's anything else remotely like Vondur'Eye. It's too vivid to think about. So it gets buried, deep as you can. But it lurks. Too powerful and consuming to stay at the fore.

So now these nero-kids are asking about it? And they've got me in The Truth.

I thought when the summons came through, it would be about the accident – so-called – on Callistone Orbit last trip out. But I got nothing to hide, shouldn't be too worried. Never been to a Truth before. Thought it would be an experience. I done nothing wrong. Should be alright. Had a friend, and another guy I know in the works. They'd been. One came back grey. The other didn't.

But I should be fine. Wasn't really involved in the accident – merely a close-by witness.

But they're asking me about Vondur'Eye. Not the accident.

'Yes,' I said. 'I know what's meant.' There. One question answered truthfully. Two to go. Then I'd be dead. And then they'll know.

Nobody talks about it, The Truth. But you know what it is, in an ominous sense. Three questions while you're laid out, and wired up. You answer true, or you die – automatic. Three questions that you must answer.

I always imagined the blade, or needle, or smother pad would be poised over me.

Admitting I knew was nothing really. Vondur'Eye was something most everybody knew of. Or had an idea what it meant – The Secret of Vondur'Eye. Oh Lordy Deesel Hai. They're probing into that? Vondur'Eye? How did they learn about me? All the others are dead. I'm the only one now.

So. I gaze up from the coacher. Dark blue above me. Points of light. Nothing especially evocative of anything. Some starfield somewhere, I guess. Not a guillotine or crush-hammer. Gas nozzles, perhaps? I wonder.

The voice is readying itself. I just heard an intake of breath. A pause. Summoning-up for the biggy. 'Do you know the secret itself?'

What? Is that the next question? I thought I knew which question must be coming next. I'm surprised at the shock of my reaction inside. Just to suddenly have to think of it. From nowhere, these questions about Vondur'Eye. The secret. The untold. I'm lying on the padding, and shaking at the memories that waterfall over me. Hai Kuut! The images that are flashing and whispering, gnawing inside me... that drool and roar. Surely, they *can't* want to know? Not *that?*

I have to answer. Or be dead. No idea how they'll kill me. But I bet it won't be a satisfyingly warm fade-away. But I can *not* tell them the secret. It's *my* yoke. If I was to tell them, they'd go there, and learn it for themselves, and take on their own chains. If I don't tell them, and they kill me, they'll know, and they'll carry my burden from the moment of my death. They really wouldn't ask if they realised that.

'Yes,' I say, 'I do know the secret.' *The blade will be hovering, poised in the blackness.* Damned Governa – the power they have. And they wield it whenever they feel the urge. As questions go, though, they aren't much cop. Surely, they could have asked one that assumed I know – seeing as they obviously believe I do. Or at least suspect I do. I'd never heard that they were merely yes/no questions and answers. Surely, they could have asked something more demanding and revealing?

The voice spoke again. Its third question. The ultimate one. 'Can you take us there?'

'Will you?'

'Where is it?'

'What is the Secret of Vondur'Eye?'

Deesel Hai! That's the one you should have asked straight away – 'What is the secret of Vondur'Eye?' That should have been first.

But it hadn't been. 'Yes,' I say, answering their third question. 'I could take you there if I had a ship, but I wouldn't, anyway.' *Stupid waste of your three questions. And if you don't know where it is, I'm not telling you. You're amateurs at this. You finally ask what it is on the sixth question.* 'I've answered the three that I must.' I tell them. 'No more.'

I wait for their furious axe to fall... the world to fade. And pass the burden on to the person behind the voice. But nothing, for a long, long time.

What the jui'ick are they doing?

Maybe they're just realising how badly they've screwed the questions up – after how much planning? Or just preliminary, off-chance fishing? So, what now? This merely confirms that I know, but they must have realised that before. They know I can take them there, and I told'em I wouldn't.

Can they force me? Or try? They're Governa people. They can do anything.

Except... I don't care what they do. I'd rather be dead than go anywhere near Vondur again, much less look into The Eye.

So I'm lying here, as if suspended in a smoke bath, waiting for something.

They must be comprehending... deciding.

I'm going to die any minute, now I've refused. Will they torture me into it? I don't care. Well, I care about being tortured, but, even after all this time, I'm never going back. Whatever they do. Glimpse into The Eye? One hundred sixty-six dead on that encounter. One survivor – me. I peeked into The Eye, and I lived. I feel dead often as not, but the others didn't live at all. Most of them didn't even stare into it.

On the rare occasions when it comes high into my conscious mind, I think of it like it was The Eye that gazed into us.

I'm not doing it again. If they let me outa this place, then I'm right out of here. Off-planet; out-system; somewhere fringe and non-Humanic. This is not going to catch up with me again. Not ever. I need to move anyway; I've been here forty-some years. That's beyond my usual max in one place. I need to cover myself better. Maybe they got onto to me through some age thing, a discrepancy – I look the same as ever. I've been too careless.

After all this kuiking time, they find me?

Maybe it'd be best for me if they kill me. But I'm not taking some Governa expedition anywhere near there.

The way I work it out... the best I can figure it, I'me sentenced to live one hundred sixty-four more lifetimes. Average life expectancy? One-twenty years? All heaped up inside me. To live through, one after another after another, like the last two that seemed endless. Sure as The Pit, I don't want to add *another* ship-full of lives to my sentence.

CONTROL

'Someone is stealing.' Ghiu, the over-boss for this section of the cargo port was determined to do something about the situation. 'It needs to be dealt with. Soon. You female humans have so little control over the males. Pyath-knows how you connived your way into a position where you've got this kind of responsibility.'

I tightened my metaphorical knicker-elastic, 'You've come down to the transit bay to tell me this? When we're in the middle of unloading a container carrier from Cordoh? It's been waiting three days already with a vacuum-null-grav-sensitive cargo that really needs to be down on the planet surface asap – today.'

He gave me the dead-on-delivery look that some glitty-eyed Tyhols have. It's not a good look, so I gave in, told my Number Two to do the Hexag boxes next, and gave Ghiu my half-attention.

'Okoi, *Sir.*' I find it's best to be polite to the Tyhols – they're sticklers for rank and status, recognition of their place. Aliens, eh? Worse than men. Lot like we humanics in many ways, mentally. Not so similar physically, with their flexi-feelers – their armas, as they call them – and glitter-blob heads. But we shared work around the port, the loading and unloading of detail or bulk goods.

He managed his crews of Tyhol labourers, and I had four dozen humans. Mostly humans, anyway; a few Tyhols and a couple of Yuyucks for the heavy stuff in awkward spaces. Extra-long and strong tentac-arms are good like that; just as well it doesn't take much brains, given what the Yuyucks are like.

'There's been some stealing? My people work well together; very efficient crew. Straightforward honest, too,' I told Ghiu.

He was persistent, and suspicious of where the dishonesty might be located.

'Okoi,' I gave in, 'if you really insist, we can set up ccv, and carry out some interviewing.'

One thing he insisted on was that his own all-Tyhol crew could not possibly be involved in anything of a dubious nature. 'It must be you humans. You are out of control.'

'You should look to your own; I see what they do. You're going to insist on starting to interview us? Checking our whereabouts, including mine? You already have access to the databases. If you're doing that, I must check into all your people, as well.'

His neck ruff bristled. 'I trust all mine. It is impossible that any of mine could engage in dishonest activities.'

'I trust all my guys, too. They'll do anything for me.'

We agreed that, in the interests of equality, we would both interview a sample of each other's crews. He selected six of my people, and I began by talking with half-a-dozen Tyhols. Two admitted to previous dishonesty of a thieving nature. I deeped them – they all have the chips embedded, so it's possible to check their movements. And raise their surface honesty values if you know how to tweak the programming. Then they should be more likely to tell the truth. It can even encourage their behaviour towards the more honest activities. But none of the six Tyhols I sampled had been up to anything of late; and their location records proved it.

He admitted the same negative result for the humans and Yuyucks he'd investigated.

'Okoi, Ghui, let's monitor; see if anyone sticks out. Although,' I had to say it, 'I always doubted there's anything involving either of our crews. It's more likely to be ship crew at one end, and Import & Customs at the other.'

He flew off the handlebars, 'How dare you accuse the high-rankers of I&C? They're all H-status Tyhols.'

I'd known he would do it; they're very protective of their hierarchy – he's on the brink of status-enhancement himself, so he's not wanting to accuse them of anything untoward.

It shouldn't have been a surprise, but it was. He'd never gone this far before. I get back home – my orbit pad – and find them in there, searching.

Delving into my personal datpoints. 'So what's this, then?' Shocked they'd do it to me, I challenged Ghiu's two side-kinks, all glitter-eyes and gloom-tips. 'Are you searching. Or planting?'

They stand there and bluster, 'Yeah, well… How do we know it's not you? Have to be sure… Ghiu believes… Can't trust you off-worlders, he says.'

I looked what they were poking into on my datpoint. 'Hello. What's these? You're planting fake info on my point? That is too obvious – I can prove I was never *there*… or there… And I was on the surface when *that* batch went. So what's the game, eh? You're covering for somebody? One of your own? Blaming me? Shut me up? Blame anyone who's human?'

Yes, that was exactly it: they can't help the ends of their neck frill curling a fraction – like blushing.

'You… you…' Jlei shuffled.

'Don't be like that… We didn't…' Khao protested.

So we all went back in, found Ghiu and started off again. 'I'm not trying to blame anyone.' He was all innocence and frill curling.

'Yes. You are. You can't find anything against my crew – humans or otherwise, so you decide on me. You won't consider alternatives. Or— you have considered, and you've decided against pursuing those avenues. Scared of higher powers eh? Blame the bottom rung? Me and the other humans? I guarantee it's not them doing any pilfering; not on any scale. I'd know.'

He wasn't liking my line of reasoning; probably too accurate for comfort. 'We'll search wherever we want, talk to them how we like…'

'Not with my blessing, you won't.'

'I will; I'm taking over both crews. You can stay as under-boss, but not if you carry on like this – accusing I&C people.'

I had a drink. Shatter-shocked. After all I've done to get this right. The lower ranking Tyhols are okoi, but when they get a poke of power, it goes to their cereblobs.

'That's it, I've had enough. Ghiu betraying me like that, at the drop of a hattoo.' I took a small sip at the liquor – very small – I wanted to stay in the real world. *Time for a change*, I'm thinking. *That post as hold-boss on the Gladly Starborn is just what I need.*

I know the captain; we get along okoi. Plus, if Mikal is still Navigation on there, well, we had a thing going at one time. And they're departing in a day or two, assuming they manage to re-pack their cargo without their previous hold gaffer. I could do that, easy. A one-year contract would suit me fine; they had maybe a dozen or so planets on their circuit... 'Yes, that'll do me.'

Captain Hikes – Peet – was pleased when I vidded across to the Gladly Starborn. We'd shipped together a few times, years ago, had re-met on update events and we both came from Territh.

I vidded my Second, and filled him in on events. He was okoi with promotion; it'd be much the same for him, just a different source of orders under Ghiu, instead of me.

'Right,' I went back to the dat-points and lifted all the access blocks. Give public access to see we're innocent. I de-let both my homes, cashed in, packed a bagful of bits, and headed off towards the Gladly Starborn.

See how they feel when the workforce is really turned loose... now I've switched off the work-ethic and honesty-control that I'd added to all their locator chips.

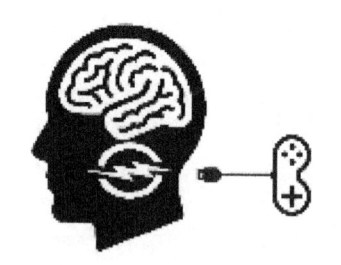

SCABBY

'You're the navigator, Raydd. You're supposed to know where we are!'

Railing at me! As if! Kopa sounds mad, but, for him these days, it's calm. Best not rise to it, especially with the other crew hanging about, ears open. 'And *you're* the commander,' I said. 'You're supposed to know where you're pointing the damn thing when you push the button.'

'*I* didn't push the button.'

That's it, Commander, deny all responsibility for what happens aboard your own craft. 'And *I* know where *I* am,' I told him. 'I'm sitting in the navigation seat at my console, exactly where I should be. Complete with screens and the navigation sphere.'

'Yeah, but where's the koiting ship?' Kopa's smooth head gleamed eerily in the greenlight of the control room.

'Hilda's hardly a ship; she's an airtight laboratory shaped like a box, converted from an over-sized Hildescar battlewagon, and over-stuffed with every kind of gear they could fit in her or latch onto her.

'Where she is in space, I have no idea.' I did my best theatrical shrug.

'She wasn't supposed to go anywhere on her own—' Second weighed in, 'especially to somewhere with no stars.' He studied the black depths of the nav-sphere. Unmollified by the view, he looked round for a face or a screen to massage his temper on.

Kopa and Second stood like the pair of plastone statues at the gates of the Imperial Space HQ – I went there once, so I know. The only two uniforms aboard – not counting my vac-faded drags, of course – Kopa no hair; Second no sense. *Perfect Top Officers.*

'It's your own fault,' I told them, 'doing a punitive task in a truly cocked-up way—' I thought they were about to descend on me, but I'm very well in with Blissen, *Owner* of the United Planetary Agency – the whole thirty-seven planets that make up the Wisp. So that gets me some leeway.

'Deg gets killed,' I carried on, 'and we import some random, hairy barbarian who calls himself King, to replace him—'

'We weren't aiming for him. He simply got in the way, and he ended up here.'

'And it nearly killed him – look at the wrecked-up state of him. I warrant he wasn't like that on his home planet.' They didn't even look embarrassed about it. 'So then Doc and Cross try to suck Deg's remaining consciousness and drop it into the imported primitive… *thing*, so they can force him to take over the unit's operation. But they also decide to have a poke round his head while they're at it.'

'Looking for a bit of pervy barbarian peep-show, you think?

'Probably, knowing them; along with being nosy about everything, anyway. But it all backfired on them. We end up with two dead experts, and a barbarian with his neurology out of tune, and his mind a mash-up of two or three other people mixed in with his own.'

'No. What we end up with is being totally lost. And three crew dead.'

There was a lot of shuffling and shrugging among the four lower-rank crew, as well as by Kopa and Second.

'Testing the matter transfer capabilities of the i/o unit was never guaranteed safe, not in a semi-mobile system like Hilda.'

'Yoiking great cylinder lying down there,' Kav joined in, 'filling what used to be the stores. Never liked the idea of it. Huh – stores on demand, instead of on the shelves.

'Nobody likes or trusts it; but it's part of *our* level of travel around the Wisp nowadays,' I pointed out.

'Blissen using us to tighten his grip on all the planets, huh?'

'Of course, but he *does* own everything, remember? He pretty much leaves places alone most of the time.'

'Sure, like the last one – Cronin? One of his little interference assignments that went *so* wrong.'

'It was us who havocked the place up, and screwed-up the job. *Us*. Not Blissen.' I stick up for him when I can. 'Besides, you all know I was on the awareness team while the mobile version of the i/o unit was being developed. We all had more than an inkling that, if the unit wasn't anchored down to the mass of a planet, there might be a way to configure it so the whole thing was transferred, instead of its contents. Which would make it an instant-drive unit for the vessel it was bolted into.

'It's experimental. We were all aware of risks. So stop whining. We now have no idea where the unit has taken us, and no-one who knows how to operate it, except maybe a barbarian from some unheard-of planet a light-yonk away. He don't speak Stang, is hairy-faced, badly out of neuro-phase, and keeps vomiting all over Chix. But just maybe, he knows how to operate the unit.

'He'll be lucky to survive the night,' I told'em. 'So what you going to do with him now?'

'We'll pump him full of juju-juice—'

'Doc and Crossy already did that, plus they embedded the language chip; then the ones they'd made for the transfer unit – which they'd put together out their own minds – and we all know what an insane— I mean, how *quirky* Crossy could be. So the barbarian's got that to contend with, as well as Deg's murdering ways; and a way-out-of-synch snatch through the i/o unit—'

'Koh, yeah. Right to all that, but *now*, we need to force him to operate us out of here.'

'Oh, for Pit's sake! We've all seen what he did. Black Angel was swinging her gun ports on us. She's supposed to be on our side! UV ranging points locked on. What did you lot do? Yoik-all. Amid all *your* panic, this barbarian calmly perused the banks, screens and consoles, and tapped in a sequence... code or something... pushed a button, and held it down for a slow count of about ten.'

I looked round them – Kopa and Second in uniforms; Chix and Vitl, the diminutive Sarrits, in work drags, the same as Kav and Stef – both with attitude – Kav with balls, Stef with boobs the same size. Plus me – sort of officer, sort of uniform; neither one you'd recognise, though.

'Whatever it was, he sure seemed to know what he was doing, and it did the dick – we were out of there in ten-time flat. And we appeared in a different *here*. You were glad of it then.'

'Yeah, but, you say we're definitely out the Wisp?'

'We're probably between spiral arms; with no idea which direction we took.'

'So here we are? Wherever *here* is. We have a matter transfer unit that maybe did what it didn't say in the manual – transferred itself, us and Hilda, instead of its contents; plus a barbarian who promptly vomited all over Chix, and collapsed.'

***

Almost entertaining, really. It hasn't endeared him to anyone, but Kopa and Second daren't airlock him, as he acted like he knew what he was doing with the i/o unit. 'We need the barbarian. If he dies, which of you is going to risk having that memo set pumped into you? considering it was drained out the brains of Doc and Mad Crossland – and probably caused their deaths? And you'd probably get Deg's nasty vindictive, murderous little mind, too. So which of you is going to opt for that way out?'

Kopa ranted. Second raved. They had to calm down eventually. 'Right. That koiting unit either destroyed the rest of the universe, or it moved us. We suspect the latter, but neither he nor us has any idea where.

'He's from a trillion yonkles away: outside the Wisp, the Empire, and all the independent confederations. He has no idea where anywhere is. He told me they have no history of interstellar travel, so nobody'll be coming to rescue him. Remember, we have no idea what that unit can do. It's *alien*-designed. It's why Blissen moved it off-planet—

'Yes, yes. We've been through that. But, face it, that unit harnesses koit-knows what power, and the first thing it actually did different was when that glass-eyed barbarian pushed the right buttons. So maybe, he does have some pre-learned techno-skill—'

'I think he said he designs computer programs and hardware.'

'Whatever that means.'

'Well, whatever, it merged with Doc and Crossy's knowledge of the i/o unit? Yeah, right.'

'Well, Blissen's got to be pleased that *something* happened.'

'No,' I interrupted their arse-oriented bickering, 'I know Blissen; he needs it to happen where he can still see it; not the far side of nowhere.'

Second shrugged again, 'So it's not Blissen's lucky day. So what now?'

***

Helpless was the word of the hour, along with shrugging.

'I'll see if I can figure out where we are,' I said, 'Let me spend time with the navvy sphere. And the cams from the i/o room. I'll also try to talk with the barbarian. See if I can figure things out.'

'Fair enough, Haik' Kopa agreed with me. That must be a first, and used my familiar name in front of the crew. 'You do your navvy thing. Stef. Kav. Downtime – power-sleeps, foods and drink, whatever. Chix… Vitl… work on our temporary crew member.'

'Koh,' the two Sarrits nodded, 'we'll see what we can do with that vomiting, shuddering, uncoordinated mess.' They're very unforgiving about vomit. And they're Hilda's medics.

***

Ah – Camera i/o 4 – there he is, pacing round, muttering. Ughh… naked; patches of body hair, like an animal. And vomit – horrible-looking thing, staggering like a drunk. Looked to be in pain. Stomping and cursing round the cylinder and the consoles, head stuffed with three dead weirdies.

Yoiks – you got to admire somebody who can survive that lot. What the koit happened to the i/o unit getting you here, huh? Something was way out of phase… made you the same, eh, Barbarian? Whatever killed the others, you survived it. Right, let's see where this's going…You're shaking like a Pinxy bride at noon. Staring at the controls and pads, readout screens and hand pads. Lips muttering… Eyes flickering between the i/o cylinder and the control consoles.

Ah. There. You just saw Black Angel ranging her fireports on us…

Other crew… yelling at him and the screens and the i/o unit. And he suddenly started sequencing things and pushed the Go button.

Koh… right. The tenth time of watching revealed nothing new.

'So where is he now?' I called to one of the crew. 'What state's he in?'

'Crewroom,' Chix came up. 'Unconscious. He was jabbering, rambling, so we sleep-induced him. And you still have no idea where we are?'

'None at all.' I shrugged. 'Well out the Wisp. No-one'll find us here, including Black Angel. Can't establish a fix on anything. Look at it.' I pressed my hands over the navvy sphere again to manipulate the internal image. 'Here. See? Nothing.'

I let'em peer, and peer a bit more. They wouldn't understand anything, anyway. 'So send us somewhere else,' Kav said, 'have a look round and see if you recognise any star patterns.'

'What? If we don't recognise anywhere, we simply keep trying again and again? We could end up anywhere.'

'We already have,' Kav and Stef laughed. 'And it don't matter where we are now, if we can't get where we want to be next. The freak is the only one who knows how to power-up the i/o unit and direct Hilda anywhere.'

'Right, and he's a frugged-up physical and mental mess – body and brain functions severely disturbed.'

'And he calls himself *King*, of all things?'

'And he isn't being cooperative now? What a double-barrelled fart he turned out to be.' Second flexed his fists, no doubt in anticipation of beating some teamwork into the semi-carcass on the bunk.

'He's *not* being uncooperative, Second. He's at Death's Gateway.'

'Be alright when we get back to the Wisp—'

'Hold it!' Stef's voice penetrated the whole wagon. 'Back to where? Blissen just tried to blow us out the vac and back. There's no way I'm going back to The Wisp if Blissen's feeling irate.'

'Koh, koh. Enough.' Kopa quelled the mutterings of agreement. 'Raydd – Haiku – keep going on finding out where we are. You two, get that barbarian awake and fit to answer questions. All of you, I'll listen to opinions about where we aim for when we know *if* we have any choice and control. Koh? *Go.*'

Kopa had spoken, so everybody shrugged and sloped off.

***

So there was me, alone again with my navvy console and globe. I stroked its smooth sphere. Scarcely a single point of starlight; nothing recognised by the system. *King doesn't know where we are. But. I saw more in his face. Maybe a twinge of Doc's deviousness? or Crossy's wappiness? Something in him knew what he was doing.*

Maybe not entirely consciously. More in survival mode than suicidal spite? I hope he didn't absorb too much of Deg's vicious streak.

Definitely not some fluke; he knew the technicalities of what he was doing, if not the entirety of the consequences.

***

Two intensive days going over the i/o unit and the navigation sphere, and running calculations through the banks. Talking with him – him trying to understand, or pretending to. Both of us touching things, stroking them, staring at screens. He ran fingers over the cylinder controls and consoles, muttering and nodding. Maybe he was genuinely attempting to string it all together, but, after a time, he'd go blank-faced, vomit and/or pass out. Yes, a combination of coming through the i/o cylinder; plus being stuffed with two raging brains, had done for him, alright.

Second was all for trying his usual fists and finger-twisting routine, but eventually realised that King wasn't deliberately buggering us up. 'Frugg him,' he told me.

Even I tried shaking him about, up here at the navvy ball. 'I watched you: you stabbed those keys too purposefully to resort to shrugs now.'

He pretended to ponder deeply and meaningfully; 'Don' know – not remember. Clear then – mixed now. This is Stang I speak?'

'Barely,' I told him. 'Your accent's from Planet Weirdo.'

'Don' know where that is…' And he'd faded back to unconsciousness. Smiling bastard. Wherever he'd been snatched from, the journey had mashed him up, totally: nobody could pretend to be that frugged out.

Standing over him, I felt like giving him a couple of kicks, but why lower myself to Second's level? *Huh, you might be a near-animal, but you make me uncomfortable; there's a pitsofalot in there, huh?*

Wait! Wait! I know! I know what you said – you told me. I didn't... Yes... I can work it out... which direction. You pointed to the cylinder's axis.

Yes. We went that way. Not the direction Hilda was facing. Because the cylinder's not positioned the same way. It's sideways, not forwards. I can figure this. Hilda's positional logs... timings... trial and error... greater and greater distances... increasingly expanding angle of direction... We were completely out the Wisp within the first second. Into unknown dust-shrouded space, invisible from the Wisp planets. A black void. Fruggit. Frugg you, King.

***

'I know where we are,' I reported back. 'I'm a genius. I been awake three shifts on the slide. Plus sheer luck. Worked out the direction from our slowly-untangling friend; expanded out and away; and kept delving deeper and deeper into the navvy-sphere's depths looking for a match on max gain, and went through every hex in there, one by one. See... *here*.

'Some Empire Deep-Space Survey craft must have drifted through here, centuries beyond its remit, long before The Wars. It must have registered *this* triple-star group as a unique way-marker – a KeyPoint – and automatically beamed it back to GeeCee. A kind of future-proofing against any future craft getting very distantly lost.'

'Like they knew we were coming, huh?'

'Might as well have. See? Completely unknown; uncharted, apart from a single drone maybe a millennium ago. Any further and we'd be in intergalactic space. However, *this* triple-group matches precisely. We have travelled very nearly a thousand light years, in fourteen point two seconds. That Pit-born creature's brain is meshing Doc and Crossy's thinking together more and more—'

'Poor sod, no wonder he's puking and mad.'

'—merging with whatever he had in there before. Plus a Stang language cryst they tried to blast into him.'

I spun round – bit theatrical, I know, but it cleared them all back a bit. 'From what he said to me – and it's not easy to tell what he's saying because it's partly in some other language, plus jargonic techno terms. He also has an accent to kill yourself to escape from, and he keeps passing out. Just the same, I believe he now re-understands the propulsion capability of the i/o unit. I think what he said was that it's like a generator-motor unit: depending how you configure it, it can be a drive unit, or, in reverse, as it were, a matter transmitter – i/o – input/output.

'If he really understands it, it's brilliant!'

'Brilliant? What? Him or the unit?' Stef obviously didn't believe any of it.

'Both. Think what it means – travel *that* fast. It's unbelievable. Black Angel's speed is incredible enough, but this thing is virtually instant. Must be some totally radical principle that Blissen, Doc and Crossy were investigating.'

'Yeah, right,' Stef sneered. 'We lose Deg, and they try to replace him, but accidently grab this barbarian.

They try to make the best of it, pump him up, Stang him; try to suck-see his mind. Except it backfired on them, and they got themselves sucked out and mashed up.'

I imagine I was the only one who cared – I knew Doc and Crossy well, and liked them, though they were dedicated pains, inconsiderate, wappy and totally self-absorbed, which equalled unpopular with the crew.

'So how's he going to get us out of here?' Kopa wanted to know. 'And how fast?'

'And where to? Not the Wisp.'

I shrugged, 'Whichever, wherever, King's the key to this whole thing. So let's have nothing slipped into his food, no neck-wire, no airlock, hmm?'

How can they be so dim-brained? All arguing about petty details, like their own lives. Blissen needs this King creature. The Wisp needs him, regardless of what went on with Black Angel.

'Look – we've seen the vids. He saved us from our Primary Problem. Problem Two? *I* solved: I know where we are. Problem Three: however rattled Blissen might be with us over whatever he thought was going on aboard Hilda, he'll welcome us back with this barbarian's brain intact. Think about it – we travelled a thousand lyres in fourteen point two seconds. It's impossible! What Blissen would do to get his hands on him.'

'No,' Stef wasn't letting it go. 'Problem Three is how we get *anywhere*.'

'Simple. We make King do it.' Second with his fist-flexing again.

'Memo-drain his head.'

'And drop it into one of you lot?'

They thought about that again. 'He understands far more than I do about that unit – the details, deep inside. More than Crossland or Doc—'

'He's too dangerous to keep alive. A quiet thong round his throat in the middle of the night would put a stop to all this...' One-track Second, we call him.

'How many times! Without him, we're going nowhere. Look, whyn't you all take it easy for a shift? Give me more time with him, and I'll see if he remembers enough to show us how to return to the Wisp, hmm?'

'Or Empire territories.'

'Or one of the Independents.'

I was seeing a deeper stratum, too – I've always been Blissen's Man-with-the-Ideas. The Blissen Link. It's me who has the solutions, the short cuts, the instant remedies. Now this King thing – a stray from The Pit – worked out the solution to the Unit's propulsion mystery in moments – after the team on Discovery spent ten years at it.

So. My role is to keep close tabs, buttons and bows on King. He's the answer. With fortune, and the stars on our side, I'll get us back to Blissen, Discovery and the Wisp in one piece.

Jeemus – How long's it been? One-hundred-twenty-five years now since I first heard of any of those?

As long as King and I survive, I don't care about anyone else. He'll do the getting us back to Discovery, and I'll smooth our way in with Blissen.

One-twenty-five years? Oh, yes, I know exactly where my loyalties lie, and it doesn't include going anywhere near the Empire or the Independencies.

***

So long ago. So far away. In Central Empire territories – GeeCee itself, where I started…

Bit more than one-twenty-five years ago… one-forty-odd… one-fifty, must be.

That first ship was everything I'd craved, The Red Jacket. Big, beautiful and brand new. I'd just received my commission; so proud of my first posting in the Empire Space Navy – the Essny. Me! From one of the less wealthy families on Plutos; youngest son of five, so it was the Space Navy for me. 'There's the Recruiting Office, son. Goodbye. No – not "See you later." It's "*Goodbye* and don't come back."'

My first voyage, we were heading out on a mop-up sortie. The Red Jacket was the Prime Ship in a squadron of five. I was First Navigation Officer, but pretty raw, newly appointed, risen rapidly through the grades because of supposed war casualties. Eight deccas out, I noted an intense gravity anomaly in open space dead ahead. 'Captain Bliyork, sir, I most extremely strongly recommend a detour around it.' My exact words.

Captain Bliyork refused to disturb Admiral Foxt for permission to alter course. 'Not coyking likely.' He practically had me by the throat. 'The admiral is renowned for keeping a strict and tidy fleet formation. "A straight line to the enemy is the only line," he'd say. He's not too well versed on the *curved* nature of space-time.'

I had everything crossed and eyes shut. We went in with five ships and came out with four. The Solly Gimlet had vanished. *So relieved. It wasn't us.*

All hushed up at the time, naturally. Wartime censorship during the undeclared mopping up period, long after The Wars had purportedly ended. We were supposed to be quelling rebellious and marauding colonies that hadn't accepted the truce, even a hundred years later. I know better now; it was GeeCee that hadn't accepted the end of The Wars of Rights. Imperial forces were continuing a covert war of attrition and consolidation, under the pretence of helping neighbouring systems against pirates. It was a much depleted and under-funded Imperial Navy from what it had been in its nova days, but it was still powerful with its old cruisers, korfrets and ten-weights. And they didn't like to lose a new four-weight korfret just like that.

Even with all the hushing up, they had to blame someone. It was standard regulations practice that sleeping admirals of the fleet never took any blame. Nor did captains of Prime Ships. Navigators did. Especially new ones straight out of Training Acad.

'It is self-evident where the fault lies,' I was told. Oh, yes, I wore the yellow flag for that incident. You don't lose an Imperial space ship with eight hundred crew, at the cost of a colony planet's annual taxes; not without paying.

It was made very obvious at the Empire Board of Enquiry: 'First Navigation Officer Raydd was fully aware of the anomaly: his memorandum said so. You have copies, my Lords.'

Yeah, right. My 'Urgent Recommendation for change of course' was redacted from the copy they were shown. Captain Bliyork wasn't taking any blame, especially with a fat pension waiting at the end of the mission. The fact that it was the first gravity anomaly ever to be encountered in open starless space was ignored. It was irrelevant, as was the fact that any potential danger was previously mere conjecture prior to that incident.

It hurt, my demotion. Deeply. I was a totally loyal believer in the Service, in the quality of Officers, in Justice, in the Empire. Became a little frayed, but I was determined to regain my rank.

A few years later I was Second Navigator on the escort vessel Fly – smart little Gun Class vessel. We were accompanying a troop transporter and a mine-sweeper/layer into the Veriden twin-planet system. My own specific role was to give practical instruction to a newly qualified First Navigation Officer, just out of his memocryst induction.

Pensell Glenvelle, a younger man, had the senior rank, and he usually overrode my instructions. 'When I want your coyking help in deploying a thousand Imperial troops, Raydd, I'll coyking-well ask for it. Until then, I think my training memo is rather more recent and accurate than yours, don't you think, mm?' Glenvelle's nose positively flared when he was being haughty. He waved his left hand about theatrically, too, and exaggerated his GeeCee accent.

The role of the Fly was purely pictorial. Three ships looked much better than two. There was no chance of resistance from either of the two planets they were headed for. The system had capitulated many years ago, all its ships confiscated or destroyed, and no others had been permitted to be built. Our whole operation was intended to be intimidatory, with the sweeper clearing a known swarm of hundred-year-old orbiting mines that Empire forces had set as a deterrent long before. Then we would re-lay them elsewhere, as a deterrent to someone else. A large occupation force would be landed from the troopship, with a high visual profile role, rather than an active engagement one.

I tried to discuss the principles of putting three ships into parking orbits in these conditions with my trainee officer. Dear Pensell had a wonderful way with being dismissive, 'I've been on a course on exactly this subject, full memo on it just recently. No need to run it through the banks, eh? So silence, hmm, Raydd?' The First Officer had duly made his calculations for the pattern and orbit, and set them into motion. Routinely, I checked the calculations, and pointed out the error. Two digits accidentally transposed.

He was outraged that I, criminal scourge of the spaceways, should dare to check his figures. 'Based on the latest memo techniques, Dear Boy.' And have the temerity to question their accuracy, and dare to demand an alteration to official data. He had me removed from the bridge. Arguing, shouting and pleading, I wasn't prepared to allow another ship to go down because I lacked the courage to stand up for what I *knew* to be right.

It took four huge guards to drag me away. 'Remain in your cabin. *We'll come for you later,*' one grinned, rather chillingly.

Three hours later, as our small fleet was sweeping into orbit around Goldring, in a neat pattern, I managed to lock myself in an escape capsule, praying that its heavy shielding would be invulnerable to the impending disaster.

Must have been quite a sight, the troopship Occupation slamming into the first of nine Imperial mines that the sweeper had come to collect. I probably wouldn't have liked the sight of it hitting the next eight as well, and the fire that engulfed the whole ship, completely gutting it, resulting in a huge explosion that blew the rear section apart and sent debris spinning in all directions.

I also missed the sight of the Miner Gravel Path desperately manoeuvring to avoid a major section of the troopship as it spun towards them. The glowing port engine struck the mine-sweeper just forward of the control bridge, causing the tail to lift, then turn end over end, slowly, nudged off course, crippled, and dipping into the atmosphere at full throttle. The sight was apparently very spectacular from the ground. The descent of the Gravel Path lit up the evening sky in a long fiery column before succumbing to the pressure and heat, and vanishing in an enormous violet flash.

***

Empire retaliation against the planet's treachery was inevitable, immediate, and overwhelming. War surplus planet crackers were scattered from an eightweight destroyer a couple of deccas later. One cracker was dropped on the sister planet, Orcan, for good measure. A few thousand people survived on Orcan. No-one did on Goldring, of course.

***

I was found hiding in the escape module, then found guilty of desertion in the face of the enemy. Then found myself in a four by three steel cell. The fact that the charge could only be brought in time of war – and the war had theoretically been over for a century – was dismissed as irrelevant. I had clearly attempted to alter the course of the vessel. I was not the First Navigator, nor was I the captain. Obviously guilty. And attempting to desert in an escape capsule! Unquestionable cowardice. The fact that the escape capsules no longer had engines or disengagement mechanisms, was also totally irrelevant. I was 'Clearly complicit in an enemy plot to destroy the fleet, and it was only by the superb ship-handling by Captain Aline and First Navigator Glenvelle that the escort destroyer had avoided destruction herself.' Both men were to be promoted to posts in larger craft.

'The lying traitor Raydd will be executed by the time-honoured method of expulsion from an airlock in a one-decca suit.' That was a bit of a downer, but hardly a shock – I was learning about *Command* and *Empire* by then.

***

It wasn't exactly at the last second that I was spared, waiting to be pushed into the airlock. They had the wrong time for dawn in an orbit at this height, so there was still an hour to go when the shuttle craft pulled alongside. From it, a very senior officer entered the airlock and came through. My guard squad jumped to attention. I had no interest – his arrival wasn't going to delay my doom by even a minute if the airlock party was cleared with its usual efficiency.

Big surprise. It was me he wanted to see – Admiral (R & D) Four Stars Regilait. He came straight to the point. 'Where, exactly, Raydd, is the gravity anomaly that you drove that fleet into four years ago?'

Set me back a little, that did, but I was learning fast, and couldn't possibly remember just like that. And why should I?

It was almost amusing. Admiral Regilait expected full co-operation there in the airlock, before I was expelled.

'But dash me, Raydd-You-Traitor. Do one decent thing before you die, and tell me.'

He was so disappointed that I was unable to give him a precise answer there and then, or even reasonably accurately. What course, what speed? Oh, yes, I was catching the first ultra-cautious glimpse of a way out; a postponement, at least. I admitted that I might just be able to work out where we had been, but it would be difficult and very time-consuming and what about the other navigators in the fleet at the time?

Two seniors were dead. Another was untraceable. The juniors never knew where they were: they were in the habit of leaving it all to the First Navigator on the Prime ship.

'A course is a course, not a place,' said one.

'Merely a set of digits,' said another.

'We don't keep hard copy of every journey on active service,' said a third.

'Who pays attention to the bit between here and there?' repeated the first. 'We just go, and get there.'

'They are being disciplined. So only you, Raydd can possibly know.' Oh yes indeed, it was coming to me most rapidly, for an officer who never previously had cause to be devious, manoeuvring, lying and crooked. I was beginning to plot my way out very clearly.

Admiral (R & D) Regilait was desperate. As soon as he found that he could not simply collect a set of precise co-ordinates from me, and wave goodbye from the airlock, he was wide open to suggestions and covert blackmail. I greeted his every appeal with absolute enthusiasm, including all his hints about possible military uses for a wandering Black Dot. 'We must do whatever we can to find it, Admiral,' I said. 'But I'm only a Second Navigator, defunct, and about to be expelled…'

***

Sure, I can smile about it now – although there's not a lot to smile about in Hilda at the moment. Control room's quiet, dull green lighting. Screens mostly off. Navigation sphere virtually blank. Yes… I have to smile about the game we played back then, all the juggling and hinting that went on between me and the admiral.

I hadn't dared to openly demand a reprieve. I still held the Service in some awe, but I held the value of my own life in some awe, too, especially with its imminent end. So I wasn't giving anything away without a corresponding concession from the admiral.

'Well, you can come inside, bit of a stay of execution while you plot it in on the ship's banks, eh?' Regilait thought he was doing me a favour.

'Actually, I was hoping for a longer stay of execution.' I gave him my most innocent look, him resplendent in his red and gold uniform, me in an out-of-time suit with all the insignia removed. 'More of a cancellation, actually. The incentive to really think hard, try my very best, you know.'

Of course, Admiral Regilait wasn't so thick that he didn't know what I was up to. He disapproved of blackmail, and only agreed because he routinely lied to staff and everyone else around him. He had no intention of giving a pardon to a convicted criminal who had wilfully destroyed three Empire Ships of the Fleet – more than the entire Doublin colonies in eighty-seven years of conflict.

But, hey! I was escorted from the airlock, reinstated as a Full First Navigator, all rights and ranks restored;

pension and experience pay replaced. Admiral Regilait duly completed the restoration form, taken straight from the ship's banks, and he signed in his best flourish, adding DOC after his signature.

Those initials merely confirmed my intentions: I knew what they meant – Death On Completion. I'd be back in an airlock soon as. I suppose my signature was rather shaky, in the circumstances, but I completed it with a set of initials of my own, AYT. The Admiral scrutinised it for a moment, and gazed back at me, suspicious, but he didn't question the AYT on the end. It obviously didn't matter to him what I was signing, as long as he found out all about the gravity anomaly from me. He wouldn't have been so smug if he knew that it stood for "After You, Turd-brain." No way I'd still be around at the end of the mission.

***

Three deccas later, I was the Honorary First Navigator on board the escort Five-weight Destroyer Fanny F. Flan. The commodore who chose the name of the ship had done so as part of the traditional retirement procedures. It was the custom to allow the most senior retiring officers to choose the name for the next ship to be commissioned. He picked the name because of a bet. It was more of a bribe, actually, from a very wealthy merchant trader, Augupine F. Flan in honour of his wife giving birth to a son and heir. The un-named ex-commodore lost his pension on a hitherto unheard-of technicality that someone discovered very shortly afterwards. The bribe, however, had been *very* substantial, and he was more than happy, especially with the fame, or notoriety, which put him in more demand on the televids than his previous sixty-year career had ever done. For the space navy to refuse the name, or to change it, was unthinkable. "The ship is the name; the name is the ship. The name could not be changed any more than the ship could be dismantled and re-assembled as a Ten-weight Dreadnought Plus."

The name was of supreme indifference to me, but the officers and crew took it very seriously. Although it was the least popular posting in the Imperial Navy, they took pride in the name, making a virtue out of necessity. So I began to refer to it as the Effin Flan, and was not popular on the control bridge. So they ignored me; avoided me; and didn't care where I was most of the time. I rather liked Mr. Augupine and his bribable ex-contact in the Navy.

The Fanny F. Flan was escorting the Imperial R & D Ship Micron Worlds, which was packed with instruments, and boffins to operate them. I recalled all the details of the original course, including two correctional changes of direction that had been too small to need authorization. I had more cause to remember than most. And I guided our two-vessel fleet with absolute precision. As soon as the instruments began to register the gravity anomaly, speed was reduced progressively until, with considerable jockeying of position, our two ships were able to take up a relatively stationary orbit around a point that didn't appear to exist. There was no sign of anything, except via the gravitic sensors.

'The Solly Gimlet is in there somewhere,' I helped them out. 'I prefer to think of her as, "Not immediately accessible", rather than lost. I know exactly where she is.'

There was much excitement aboard the Micron Worlds, as speculation centred around the apparent discovery of a neonatal black hole. As far as they could tell, there was no super-collapsed star at the centre of their orbit; certainly not the mountain-sized non-masses of the known ones; nor the GeeCee-sized ones they thought they knew about, but didn't dare go too near. And this one was in open empty space, not in a swirling hydrogen cloud, cooking under its internal strife. Nor was it buried deep within star streamers, spinning and disintegrating, sucking galaxies to their doom. This was a seed for a black hole, they believed. With nothing close by to suck in, it could remain like this for billions of years.

'Could we really get it to move towards the Falkan Dependencies?' Admiral (R&D) Regilait wanted to know. In theory, it couldn't exist, but it did, so any speculation about it, and what they might do with it, was no more far-fetched than its simple existence. The immediate intention was to guide drogue capsules towards it, or into it: to calculate trajectories and speeds: measure the intensity of the gravity field: plot the parabolas and ellipses; and decide which sensors and recording equipment to use on later attempts.

The general gossip aboard the Fanny F. Flan was more interesting: the second engineer's liaison with three much younger ladies; recent discovery of a three-headed alien species on the fringe of the Booker Group; the temporary marriage of the quartermaster to one of the gunnery sergeants; the missing ten crates of VI alcohol from the stores; the upcoming birthday celebrations planned by the weapons master; the near loss of a day's pay by Admiral Regilait – or Reggie the

Lay, as the crew called him, in recognition of his sexual appetite among the medical personnel.

My ears pricked up at the sound of Regilait's name, 'Oh, a day's pay? What for?' I asked innocently.

'Exceeding his powers,' laughed one of the cadets from the Micron Worlds. 'He revoked a death penalty.'

'Can't do it, of course. Must be a Five Star to do that. Or a committee of two Three Stars or above.'

'He was given the choice: lose a day's pay as a fine; or confer with Admiral Kenjs to confirm the reprieve; or retract the reprieve altogether. Only one thing to do, of course.' The cadets were laughing.

'Of course,' I joined in with their laughter, 'Can't go throwing money away, letting criminals get away with... whatever it was... anybody know who it was?'

No-one did.

Bit sick inside, I retired to my cabin soon afterwards. 'The bastard. I always knew it. Not even one day's pay, or a ten-minin chat with a colleague.' I permitted myself five mins of rage – the DOC signature already said it all. 'This merely precipitates matters. I need to decide what I want and how to achieve it. Surviving comes first – I didn't like the feeling in the airlock aboard the Madrigon Blue. Far better for all the others to die, if only to cover my tracks. Besides, who else would have *five* Imperial Wrecks to their credit? A brag like that would buy me everlasting drinks on any of a thousand non-Empire planets.

Time I was packing, I said to myself. *I just need to make sure I'm indispensable for the time being.*

The only other navigator aboard was a sour veteran, forced to work out his years aboard the Fanny F. Flan for his frequent incompetence due to a drink problem. I sought him out, got him paralytic drunk, hallucinating on a 4F drugs cocktail, and heading into the gravity anomaly in a passenger drogue, singing, 'It's all downhill from here,' in double-glad time.

The boffins were excited at the prospect offered by the unexpected volunteer. The crew shook their collective heads. And I was the only navigation officer left aboard. Navigator Dresht's voice began to ramble loudly and incoherently, evidently unaware of his predicament, or uncaring of it. It suddenly increased in pitch and speed, then abruptly cut off. There was absolute silence. I wondered if he had any friends who'd been aboard the Solly Gimlet – he could perhaps catch up on old times.

It was decided to move in closer, send another drogue with more instruments, and to make me the official First Navigator (Acting).

The second drogue went in, all instruments recording and transmitting. The two ships moved closer, in increasingly faster orbiting speeds.

A third drogue went in.

Then it was decided that one ship should make a close flypast. A debate ensued about which one it should be. The boffins would ideally have liked to be on the ship that went in *and* to watch it from the other one. Captain Vince-Ch of the Fanny F. Flan vetoed the use of a purely military vessel for dangerous purposes. 'I mean, *scientific* purposes,' he corrected himself.

So it had to be the Micron Worlds, much to my relief, and that of all crew of the Flan.

Ordered to check the course proposed by the navigator on the Micron Worlds, I altered the plan so that the vessel would describe a beautiful parabolic curve into the anomaly, and not come out again. I returned it with the message that the navigator's calculations were perfect. And entered a message into our own banks that the proposed course was terribly wrong and should be altered accordingly. I gave it absolute top most urgent priority, filed it away quietly, and carried on loading provisions into the escape craft I had ear-marked for my personal use.

The curve into the black dot was exactly as I planned. The squealing voices cut off at precisely the predicted time. 'Four,' I sadly congratulated myself, adding the Micron Worlds to the Solly Gimlet, the Occupation and the Gravel Path. And shortly to include the Fanny F. Flan. An enviable haul of Empire vessels by any standards.

The speculation aboard the Fanny F. Flan decided that the boffins had been carried away by their own enthusiasm, wanting to experience it all for themselves, to see it from the inside. I reluctantly reinforced that view when I produced my message, strongly urging them not to take the proposed course. I was most pleased that Admiral (R & D) Four Stars Regilait had gone with them, complete with his day's pay. I hoped he wouldn't pop up in some tenth dimension, future time, alternative universe, or whatever, and wreak vengeance on me. It was just a touch worrying that a *negative* gravity anomaly had been reported somewhere beyond the Booker Group.

The fate of the Fanny F. Flan was already well in hand. There didn't seem to be any point in staying longer. If we returned to Base, I'd be executed anyway: it was on the forms, especially with this one added to my quota.

So, when I was ordered to prepare a course for Base Cresidon, I punched it into the banks, locked them, sealed the access, put in two additional safeguard passwords, and went to the main landing bay.

Bellowing loudly to the maintenance crew, 'I can't take the guilt any longer! I'm responsible!' I clambered into the main escape capsule and launched the little craft into the void, leaving behind a navigation program with a progressive one percent of error.

I swiftly re-checked the mass of provisions in the storage lockers, and the personal belongings that I'd smuggled in earlier. Enough supplies for about a year, and it would take about that long to reach Corsoff at the speed the capsule could manage.

Over the next hours, stretching to a day, I watched the rear screen as the Flan gradually began to turn away, going off course by one degree every ten minutes.

***

I often used to imagine how things went aboard her. I've built it up into a complete last-few-hours sequence in my mind…

...My sudden departure and loud admission of guilt about something would be greeted with consternation at the loss of their navigator; turning to relief when they realised that I had safeguarded their futures by pre-programming the ship to reach Cresidon. So they would have been happy. By the time Captain Vince-Ch realised that it was the Fanny F. Flan that was curving away, not the escape pod, it would have been too late.

The captain will have believed the Fanny F. Flan was altering course in order to head for Cresidon.

Then they'll have considered the possibility of an engine fault...

Then a guidance systems failure, as the vessel continued with its regular slight changes of direction.

Eventually, someone would have had the thought, 'It must be an error with the navigation systems.' But wouldn't occur to anyone that the inaccuracy had been introduced deliberately, largely because no-one on board knew how to re-program the navigation systems, even if they could get past the first password.

And all the time, the Fanny F. Flan was curving back whence she came – up her own parabola.

I always imagine the captain decided to accept the course they were on, 'It will take us somewhere,' he'll have pronounced. 'Our emergency message will be picked up when we're close to a civilized region. Merely a matter of waiting it out a few deccas.'

Right at the end, when it was evident that they were heading directly for the black dot, someone will have tried to boost the starboard engine to maximum, and switch the landboard one to full reverse. I wonder if Captain Vince-Ch's last words were, 'Well, you'd think that Raydd chappie would have had the decency to notice the error in the program before he killed himself.'

A tale I heard, many years later – one of the fables of the spaceways – was that when Supreme Empire Commodore Chapman heard the news that the Fanny F. Flan had disappeared without trace, his ungentlemanly response was said to have been, 'Thank the Pit for that. Whoever got rid of her deserves a rekking medal.'

***

Hi ho – come and go. Hilda's control room isn't exactly a hive of enterprise. Second and Kav still occupied with their weaponry checks; the others in the rec-and-rest room below. I can dream on… Stef stiffly studying one screen after another, seated two consoles along, fists clenched solidly, no apparent awareness of me.

***

I drifted in the escape pod for almost a year before I was picked up by the tramp freighter My Own, in orbit around Corsoff.

Celebrating my rescue, I drunkenly confessed to my five Empire spacecraft scores, and persuaded Captain Grass to take me on, 'My escape craft is very valuable, and the military markings can easily be erased.'

Grass had laughed, 'And when some bright Essny spark notices, then we get fried, and so does whichever planet I'm orbiting. Let's dump her into a burn-up orbit, and we'll get you down on the surface with the crew. Plenty of old merchant uniform drags you can dress in. Won't be noticed.'

We all swore to everlasting secrecy, and that was it. I was away, free. Could create a new ID anytime. Destitute, but filled with thirteen carefully worked-out plans, of greater or lesser feasibility, on how the Empire, or parts of it, might be destroyed or put to good personal use.

Didn't entirely work out that way, of course. I was in a region of slowly-recovering planets that had caught the wrong side of the Empire's military policies in the past. Years of fruitless drifting and plotting eventually took me to Orcan, whose fate I often felt guilty about. She was the sister planet of Goldring, which had been semi-vaporised around ten or twelve years earlier – depending whose years you counted in.

I was embarrassed about misdirecting a freighter that way, on the strength of rumours of a wealthy, hidden planet. But the thin sulphurous atmosphere, the scorching heat and the dying vegetation that had been created by one casually tossed planet cracker obviously wasn't a cover for vast riches below. The crustal crack extended for fully a third of the planet's circumference, and only one scattered pocket of population had survived.

Jumping ship in the emergency landing pod made me feel even more guilty, but I left all my pay credits behind – a year's money for Captain Concar to weigh against the cost of the capsule, or going down to the surface in the main lander, and trying to locate and recover his missing pod. With a full cargo of guan capsules going off in the bulk hold, and a tinker's assortment eating into his capital in the main hold, he evidently decided to continue on to a planet that had a mass lift platform. I imagine he was permanently disillusioned with the vagaries of space life, and, without a navigator again, would have pointed the White Mist III hopefully towards the Beacon, a giant twin system that halved in magnitude every six hours as one star occluded the other. Easy to locate and lock on to. He'd be koh.

***

Down on the surface of Orcan, the struggling population in the area known as Paladas greeted me with mixed feelings. I was the first non-military off-world visitor since the cracker had devastated the planet.

Their only news of the supposedly long-finished Wars, and what had happened to their once-beautiful planet, had come from the Imperial Colonial Commissioner. About five years before, there had been a fleeting visit by a party of officials wanting to confirm the neutral and unarmed status of Orcan. The commissioner had expected the planetary governor to sign a declaration admitting Orcan's complicity in plots, atrocities and armed aggression against the Empire. It was necessary for the declaration to be signed so that Orcan could not sue the Empire for reparations, for their obviously justified retaliatory action in quelling the rebellious population. Thus, the commissioner explained, the way would be open for Orcan to receive Imperial Assistance without prejudice.

Demands by the populace to know what had happened, and why, were met with blank, uncomprehending stares from the commissioner and his party. 'Why would anyone want to know such a thing? What is there to know? It was wartime, wasn't it?'

'Well, no,' the populace explained, 'it was a hundred years after the Wars of Rights had officially ended. We were peaceful, and unarmed.'

The commissioner had been sympathetic. 'It took a long time to get the peace message out to all the outlying colonies, and the military were rather enthusiastic at times. Now, please sign this declaration of guilt so that you will be eligible to receive war aid, free, apart from the acceptance of Imperial rule. Well, not free, exactly, and not rule, precisely, but a sort of loan, with an occupying force to make sure you don't go anywhere whilst the debt is owing.' He smiled the way smug Empire shits always do. 'And if you don't sign, then you're still officially at war with the Empire, and I don't know if I can hold them off much longer.'

And so the surviving pocket of Orcans created a governor's position for the planet, installed a volunteer, and had him certified officially insane. He was presented to the commissioner as Governor Lord of Orcan – Gloo. Gloo was a popular children's storyvid character who was always doing fun-poking things to pompous people. He duly signed the commissioner's silly piece of plaspap.

Not long afterwards, Imperial Colonial Commissioner Willybrand left with his party. They were delighted with their signed declaration, unaware that its signatory was officially demented, and the document was therefore invalid. He was also ecstatic with the great honour conferred on him by the grateful people. He had been given an official title whilst on Orcan, and should place the initials after his name on all official documents in future – Commissioner Royal And Pacific. It was a bit stretched, but it was the best they could do when his departure was suddenly announced.

'It now only remains,' he said in his parting speech, 'for you Orcans to irrefutably prove that any damage to the planet was wilfully caused by the Empire. And the best of luck with that,' he smiled.

'Thank you, Commissioner Willybrand, C.R.A.P.,' they replied in unison.

***

Their initial suspicion of me increased as it became clear that I knew more about the planet-destroying operation than they did. 'I heard the details from a merchantman who heard it directly from the navigator of the Fly, one of the ships that had witnessed the events at the time.'

They saw right through me, 'Whoever heard of merchantmen and military mixing socially?' and knew I must be speaking from personal experience.

The escape craft from the White Mist III was especially welcomed, particularly because it doubled as a "samples shuttle", with a small cargo space capable of carrying a few stores, people or trade goods.

Within the surviving patches of usable land around Paladas there was a large fuel depot for ground machinery, but no machines to use it, and the fuel was poor quality. With no means of travelling efficiently, the population of several thousand souls had not been able to explore or forage far. A vast side-shoot of the main cracker-induced fault had reached a few miri to the north. Fortunately, almost all the lava that welled from it had spread in the other direction. The fissures and volcanic vents were still active, and the little enclave of survivors was surrounded by an endless chaos of lava plateaux and ash fields, and chasms a miro deep and wide. Thousands of small towns and villages, and the great cities of Cobrasdan, Slinham and Falby had been overwhelmed completely by lava or deep and unstable cinderlands. The stench of sulphur and the poison of other mineral cocktails filled the air, ruining more land every year.

They'd had no contact with any other part of the planet in the eleven years since the catastrophe; no televids, radios, aircraft, nothing. Imperial Colonial

Commissioner Willybrand, C.R.A.P. had not been aware of any other pockets of survivors, and nor had I when I dropped the White Mist III into orbit around Orcan.

'There might be others,' the people of Paladas said. 'Your shuttle could let us explore beyond our immediate confines. If not survivors, we might find something else of use.'

So I made myself useful, and flew a few expeditions to the east. We found medical supplies, seeds, two tractors that had to be taken apart, and carried piecemeal back to Paladas for reassembly. A powerful radio transmitter and receiver was found and retrieved; a detox unit for soil; filters for the water; a great variety of small equipment, materials and foodstuffs. But no people, no animals, no areas of crops growing wild. As far as we could explore, the planet was desolate and virtually unpopulated.

Then one day, out foraging, we picked up the bleep of an emergency beacon...

***

I reclined my navvy seat in the Hildescar's control room – Stef still there; Kopa muttering with Second – poked under my cap to scratch my head, feeling a mite rueful at the memory of what followed that bleeping alarm. But it led me to Mar-aijja. 'Lord, she was fantastic. A beautiful slip of a thing then, and still is, and so quietly wise. Farfallina, too.' Sighing, I glanced round again: no-one was watching me particularly.

***

Simple cross referencing between pod and Paladas located the beacon about a thousand miri away to the west, over the nearby range of volcanoes and the main fissure. It would be much too far and dangerous for a land expedition. It was also going to be difficult for the pod.

But reckless me, I went, with Dee-ast in the single passenger seat, and flew over the site, surveying for a landing spot. Dee-ast, still as the official governor of Orcan, had been deemed to be the appropriate companion for me, being officially insane. He was allowed to keep the title in case the Commissioner came back, and, anyway, anyone who volunteered must be mad, so the title was appropriate – Dee-ast, Gloo.

That was when the pod started playing up; it didn't like all the atmospheric gliding and swooping, and the injectors were becoming fussy about the low-grade fuel. Attempting to clear any blockages and deposits in the lines, I took her into orbit with a single high-power thrust, as the motor was intended to be used. I buzzed it a few times, and it was certainly an improvement on the near-twenty per cent power drop of the last few hours.

We glided the pod down under minimum control, and no power until the last moment, performing a neat back-thrust and stall at the perfect moment, settling gently and impressively on the spot I'd picked out. I was impressed, anyway.

Dee-ast and I were greeted with absolutely ecstatic joy and wonderment by a group of eight women and a waiflike girl-child. Marooned whilst on a Pioneer and Wilderness Awareness Expedition at the time of the cataclysm, their number had gradually reduced from thirty, and increased by one. From pre-memotime girls, they had grown up in the intervening years, and one had given birth to a daughter, now aged nine years.

Fathered by the impetuously lustful expedition leader in expectation of imminent death when the planet cracker had been dropped, Farfallina was an elfin creature with huge brown eyes and a wise curious expression: nine going on ninety. It wasn't her real name, just something I misheard when I asked her, and it seemed to suit her, somehow. Her father, embarrassed to be alive after the initial devastation and his rapine activities, had been lost on the last reconnoitring expedition, heading south, and never seen again. All six men had disappeared or died. The girls and women had survived a little better, but had despaired of ever being found, of there even being anyone to do the finding. 'We owe our survival to daily prayers to Rheagaea, and a fluke chance which thrust this mountain block upwards. The lava's been flooding the surrounding lowlands in successive waves ever since.'

'It's getting higher and closer.'

'A few years at most.'

Even with the Pioneer Centre largely intact, life was increasingly difficult, with the lava rising, crops and animals dying, and without the strength of the missing men. 'It was only our Survival memocrysts that enabled us to keep going at all. So, when the quakes suddenly became worse, we put all our efforts into repairing and powering the beacon.'

'Paladas isn't going to be a lot better in the long run,' Dee-ast said, 'but it should last longer than this place.'

The pod snugly accommodated the nine additional passengers in the cargo bay. With the promise of a return trip for their most treasured possessions, we took off for the main settlement.

***

'Oh shuggs!' Sitting here in the warm shadows of Hilda's controls, my stomach still churns when I recall that flight. Eighteen minutes of high-power thrust, and we were struggling…

The controls weren't responding well; the motor was spluttering, and we were at nineteen thousand feete. The stubby wings began shuddering. The motor jerked in and out of phase. All my flicking and blipping, pumping and priming, stamping and heaving couldn't get the motor back to a smooth fire pattern. The last resort – cursing and swearing – didn't noticeably help, either. Moderately desperate, I dropped her into eco-mode for a long, low-power semi-glide directly towards Paladas. We managed a few more hundred miri – most of the way back – before the motor cut out.

There was no restarting it. Throughout the long glide down, I tried everything I knew to force and persuade life back into it, all the time searching the land ahead for something flat, unobscured by smoke, not strewn with boulders, free of the deep ash plains. But I was on a loser, trying to glide as long as possible over the fumaroles and sulphur vents. Pits! I was desperate: no flat areas, no solid ones, hardly even seeing the ground at all in most places.

Spotted a level tract almost dead ahead. A thou too high. Went into a steep dive rather than overshoot it. Too much speed, and no motors to kill it with. I jockeyed and juggled and fought and cursed and lined her up. Hurtling in at enormous speed, realising that the surface wasn't quite so flat after all: low hillocks and small rocks. Nowhere else. Too late. Grace itself on the controls, I lifted the nose up into a stall, felt it drop backwards. Then spinning over in an unpowered turn, and I was fighting to bring it back on an even keel, level out.

It was dangerous under normal circumstances. Without power, it was near suicidal. But the swoop and stall killed most of the speed, and we hit the ground doing not much above stall speed.

Just the same, we bounced, spun and almost rolled. Heard the skis snapping off, metal juddering and screeching like mating scrandors. Praying the base wasn't torn out of the cargo bay with all the passengers in there. Bouncing again; hit a mound, dug in, spun again, and slammed sideways into a rock face. A thousand curses jolted through my mind before a massive crashing smash silenced them. *So loud.* Glassite shattering all over me. Face. Eyes. Front screen gone in blasting spray. Side screen crashed in. Dee-ast battering into me, structural girders crushing into the cab from the hold and the roof.

Everything slamming and crashing and grinding. A lurch. A drop. Dust, smoke and ash all around. *We've stopped.* Plus the creaking, hissing and groaning of twisted and strained metal. And the stench of burning plascover and hot fuel. Overpowering.

'Shit.' The pod suddenly dropped back from its nose-down position, and I was jerked all over again. 'What a mess.'

Very gradually, I became aware of crying and whimpering, querying voices, gasping and groaning. Maybe some was from me. And my own predicament was coming to me: I was in a mess, pinned back in my seat, head trapped against the rear of the seat and the girder behind it. Neck stretched, throat exposed, breathing was difficult and dusty. Couldn't move my head, just my eyes.

Not a lot to see. A loose mass of cold red-brown lava rock was occupying most of the cab, frozen in twisted and bubbled billows. I had the front screen and the controls rammed into me. Tried to see Dee-ast... and call, but I could only croak. Didn't get any response. Reached round, arm hurt, wouldn't lift high enough to feel what was trapping my head. Something hard up there – a girder. Something soggy – my head. Very gingerly, I felt it, and decided a roof girder had come adrift, and caught me at the top of my forehead. *Frugg! I been scalped.*

I was held back by the thick layer of skin and hair that had peeled back, trapped between the girder and the rigid headrest. Blood trickling down my forehead, and ponding up in my eyes because my head was forced back so much. I remember thinking we'd never get out this damn mess. *They'll really hate me now.* Could only wait...

A face loomed close. The first of the women to prise open the cargo hatch was deeply shocked, almost hysterical, when she saw the state I was in... and she could probably see Dee-ast, too. She dropped back into the bay and gibbered to the others, then came forcing back, face swimming the other side of all the blood.

All a dream to me. Sweet, frightened face, suddenly appearing, abruptly breaking into a smile. Must have realised I was alive. I felt grumpy about that; *You shouldn't be happy about it when I feel so Pitawful shattered.*

Prying and poking round me. She knelt on the seat next to me, and it dropped a finger-length. Top of my head ripped away more and I screamed and gasped, 'N... n... nooo!'

She was more careful after that. Saw her grimace at Dee-ast. Shocked voices round me. Glimpses of movement, other faces, asking, nodding, shaking of heads, someone being sick. Helping each other out the cargo hold, stopping each other's bleeding, strapping broken arms up.

All a nightmare to me. Helpless to do anything, trapped by my scalp. Throat pulled back tight. It was pain-and-gasp time, trying not to curse and yelp. Three of the women could get close enough to put their combined strength into prising the headrest free from the girder. It was a massively strong H-shape of plasteel, twisted back by the impact, so it didn't move any more than the Farley Tower would have done. And the seat was welded into place.

'The only thing that has any give in it is you,' one of them told me. I wasn't taking it in too well – all red fog and pain for me. 'We'll have to cut off the flap of skin that's holding you there. You'll be all right.'

They didn't sound like they believed it. So I had to sound chirpy instead and tried to tell'em to frugging get it over with. They were hesitating and I was getting more and more pained and impatient to be done with it all, and my throat was near to cracking with the stretching, dust and smoke. Shocked and shaking, I only wanted to be out of there. 'Just do it,' I said.

So one of them, Mar-aijja, came at me with a small knife gripped tightly, determined look on her face, and a brief word of supplication to Rheagaea. Pressing up close, kneeling on the seat again, teeth gritted. I was determined to be strong. Not scream.

That lasted all of three beats after she started hacking at the back of my head. Both of us gasping and choking and squawking. Stopped to laugh for a moment, then hacking again. And I yowled and crushed fingers into the armrest. She hacked and grunted. 'Blade's too short... can't get right behind... it's blunt.'

She hacked frantically through my hair and skin and flesh. I felt every slice and tear and grunt for a ghastly age, till my head flopped forward with a final squurk as the last bit tore free. Eyes stinging with tears, and blocked with blood, I couldn't see anything as they dragged me out. Just a glimpse – Dee-ast. Face white, drained of blood, the girder hadn't stopped at the bulkhead behind him. It had gone right through his chest. His shoulders and head were only held up by the webbing. Bits of windpipe and collar bones and ribs hung down from the girder-burst. In the seat there was a mass of pulp and blood with a pair of legs going into it.

***

Even now, in the green gloom of the Hildescar Gunship's navigation section, running a hand over my scalp, I can recall every iota of agony. 'Pits! That was scrugging awful.' I remember coming round on bare rock, in the shade of the wrecked pod.

The women clustered around, anxious; desperate for me to recover. I'd been unconscious for a full day, and they'd used the time for recuperation and bandaging each other up. A segment of my scalp was strapped back in place, once it had been freed from its pincered prison. It sure didn't feel good.

Walking out was the only option. That much was very obvious. I had a fair idea of the direction and the distance, but not of the terrain to be covered. Before noon on the second day, I collapsed, delirious, dehydrated and derelict.

They checked me over again – a line of bruising across both shins. 'Probably fractured,' concluded Mar-aijja, who had no medical knowledge at all. But she was right, and followed her diagnosis up with a comment about me smelling. My scalp was infected, and leaking yellow poison into my bloodstream. So they ripped the remains off my head and scrubbed me up with lava rock and sulphur water. Fully scalped, they carried me out of there. I think it was me who was sobbing most.

Don't recall more than snatches of it: long and pained. They sat me up now and again, asking which way and I'd look round and try to remember, and look at the shadows for the time of day and north-south directions, and say, 'That way across the ash fields,' or, 'Through the col.' But half the time I could scarcely tell the nights from the days; or the dreams and nightmares from the reality. Howling images filled every moment, awake or asleep.

Till one night, lying cushioned in tufa debris and reeking of sulphur fumes, I was aware of a hand caressing me. So soft and warm and delicate. Becoming stronger and more persistent, more intimate. Strew! It felt good... calm... warm. I was too drowsy and pained to be startled, let it happen, vaguely aware of a smooth body and long silken hair.

Long, long moments, with no pain. I never experienced such writhing and awe before – seemed so urgent, heaving and gasping. First night without the nightmare dreams.

Next morning, I was back to weakness and zonked-out pain; and no idea which of the women it had been – if it had even been real. Mar-aijja was the one I knew best, with long hair, almost black. They were all pretty much like that, though. She was petite and energetic, and she spoke to me most often. But she didn't hint about any nocturnal activities. The only one with any previous sexual experience was, I presumed, the mother of the child, and I didn't know which she was: they all looked after little Farfallina.

I gave up wondering, as the jolting and lurching on the makeshift stretcher took over for the rest of the day.

Dreams or reality? I had no idea. Still don't. Thrashing or moaning, pain or ecstasy, until the infection began to ease away and I could take more notice of the separate individuals around me, their different faces and voices, names. Tried to walk, but I was too slow, and the going too precipitous; or deep, soft ash. A danger to everyone, they tied me to the stretcher and lowered me down, hoisted me up, or dragged me along, past bubbling mud gloops and smoking ash fields, over beds of jagged lava, and alongside pits of fiery fountains.

Succeeding nights, I was sure of different bodies, larger breasts, firmer ones; slimmer waists and stronger thighs;

longer hair, or bristly; husky whispering or kissing silence; but no names.

Days became easier. The land was becoming less smashed and volcanic; fewer choking sulphur clouds; occasional patches of sparse yellow-crusted vegetation. I walked more, and talked with the women and the delicate Farfallina. No-one ever mentioned the darkness-shrouded activities, only how I was feeling; which way we're going; 'Do you recognise that landmark? Where are you from?' How they'd lived for those eleven years; the people at Paladas, and beyond. 'What happened to cause the planet-shattering?' None of them had ever travelled off-planet, and could scarcely believe that it was possible. I chatted and guided them.

'That triple peak,' I pointed, 'I've seen it from Paladas.' We altered direction; reconnoitred a valley, and a ridge; decided on a scarp, a saddle; risking the crumbling crust of a lava flow against the depth of an ash lake; to take the chasm, or detour round the boulder field, as long as we kept the three spires in sight.

The ground became easier; arid scrub and sand, then sparse grassland, scattered trees. A cultivated meadow! Buildings, people, and help. Crowds of faces and jabbering, and food and drink and rest and a two-lurg wagon ride into Paladas. It was over.

Strange how I felt so empty amid all the joy and relief. Like I lost something of great value, but didn't know what.

I recovered over the next deccas and years. Slow: I still limp on bad days. Even had brief celebrity status; they called me "Haiku". I quite liked that; saw it as an honour for bringing the party of newcomers into the fold; didn't bother with my real given name again:

Sondor. I was comfortable with my new name, and being accepted in the Paladan community. Wedded after only five deccas, to Mar-aijja. She confessed my new name, loosely translated from the original highland Orcan, meant 'scab head'. Mar-aijja assured me that it was innocently descriptive, in the ancient way of the highlands, an honoured title for an honoured deed. I accepted it philosophically.

***

So now, I have my semi-recreational time in the Hildescar Gunship-cum-orbital laboratory, getting a bit of adventure in; helping my friend Halberr Blissen with a few Wispish matters.

Right now, it seems that I'm a thousand light years from my homes on Discovery and New Orcan. And from there, it's another two hundred back to GeeCee and Orcan.

Even after more than a century, I occasionally feel a pang of embarrassment when the crew of Hilda call me Haik – Scabby. But they don't know. My only memento from those long-gone days is this, my ESSNY cap. Even more battered and frayed than me, braid's more grease than gold now, and the blue's more sky than midnight. Still like to wear it; it gives me a touch of status – mystery – when I'm on active service. There's always someone looking to see if they can spot the join in my scalp. Plus, it's my trademark on the wagon – they expect it.

***

An expedition back to the escape pod was successful. I restarted the engines after spending a day cleaning the injectors; and we buried Dee-ast in aromatic haste. The freshly re-refined fuel had been difficult to produce and transport, but worth the effort. The pod flew like a dream, crushed cab, temporary controls and all.

***

We never discovered any other survivors on Orcan, although we didn't go too far in the pod after its reassembly. It wasn't guaranteed airtight, so I wasn't prepared to risk it at high altitudes, much less into orbit. I taught some of the Orcans to fly it – so they had options for routine low-altitude portage, and in case anything happened to me. We used it for cargo and people transport, foraging, ambulance, supplies and rescues when fresh lava flows cut outlying communities off.

All through that hard, sulphurous time on Orcan, I never once wondered why I'd come there; or regretted it. After what we'd done to the planet, it was where I needed to be.

Only once did Mar-aijja and I discuss the nocturnal activities of the trek. Tentatively at first, then freely, she agreed that she had indeed been the first, and the most frequent, visitor. But she was quite open in admitting, 'All my companions helped, and enjoyed you. Except Far-kijja, who you called Farfallina. She's adopted that name now. We refused her permission to sleep with you – her age precluded it. For the time.'

I was a little shocked, despite suspecting it all along. 'But Sondor, my little kush-vie... Haiku,' Mar-aijja reasoned, 'you needed help and distraction. We needed initiation and experience in loving. We thought it worked well,' she smiled coyly. 'Of course, Far-Kijja wasn't pleased, but we had to be firm with her.'

'Well, she was only ten,' I remember smiling as I thought of that elfin face – so bright. And she'd been wanting… sex. At that age.

'Exactly, and that's what we explained to her. There'd be plenty of time later when she was more mature and you were straightened out. She's fourteen now, and available, if you wish.' Mar-aijja had looked at me so invitingly, on behalf of the wraithlike Far-Kijja… Farfallina.

'What do you mean, if I wish?' This sounded suspiciously like an invitation.

'Oh, *she's* willing. And *I* don't mind, of course. All the girls like you, and, well, you know how things are here – pair bonding, marriage, they aren't necessarily exclusive. I know more than a couple of the girls carry a heart for you. They'd dearly like to renew your acquaintance, once I tell them you've been straightened out.'

'That's twice you've said that. Straightened out?'

'Well, you know what a fuddy you are, Sondor. I had to wait until you accepted it, the past and the future. You've kept it to yourself all this time, but now I can tell them that your eyes are opened.' She beamed at me, flicking back a stray frond of dark hair.

'Am I understanding you right? You'd approve of me, er, reliving the nights of our trek? What about you?'

Mar-aijja misunderstood. 'Oh, I shan't. You'll do for me,' smiling with that aching vision she had.

'I mean… surely, you'd object?'

'Certainly not. They're my friends; it's customary. It's always been approved on Orcan, and especially now with such a limited gene pool. It's wonderful that you're kee-vo now. I'll tell them.'

So I accepted the situation, with trepidation at first, then with enthusiasm, and finally with contentment. It was like being members of a special club, with parties and reunions, shared experiences and secrets and recollections. A whole new relaxed and fulfilled way of life began for me. All the liaisons were strictly one-offs, nothing overly emotional, no private after-times for deeper feelings to develop, though there were times when we did all meet – celebration days of all kinds – mid-summer, mid-winter, harvest, spring plant, birthdays, marriages... quite frequently, I suppose.

Then, as the women gradually took permanent partners, I tended not to continue with the dallyings after the parties, and fewer chance meetings. A few did continue, blissfully and contentedly, and several revived from time to time. Farfallina Far-Kijja was allowed to join in.

Truth to tell? I was supremely fond of her, more and more so. And she seemed to be almost in awe of me. 'She's utterly devoted, you fool.' And that was both of them telling me.

I tried several times to explain, to talk to her, to put her off, to find her a partner from the young men of the town, but she would have nothing to do with them. 'There's a good choice,' I told her. 'Five thousand population – there must be a hundred youths, young men around your age.'

She called our first child Sondorson. One day, I came in from the machine sheds, and she'd moved in with Mar-aijja and me. Been the three of us ever since.

It was a tad awkward at first, but I didn't have any choice other than to accept the situation. Farfallina and Mar-aijja were adamant about it. And I was, after a few deccas, more than utterly contented. I asked about becoming an Orcan citizen. 'Sure,' they said. 'Just say you are. That counts. Nothing to sign or exchange.'

Two children by Mar-aijja, one by Farfallina, and another on the way; at least seven or eight more around the settlement. Really, honestly, I could never have dreamed of life being so good. It was wonderful. I was respected in the community as pilot, forager and advisor to the Spokesman. And the only citizen who'd ever been off-planet. And I'd helped to bring in the last stragglers from the Burn-lands.

***

'See that new star? Low, towards the setting sun?' I pointed the others towards it.

'What of it? Meteor or something? Comet?'

'It's a ship in orbit. Could have been there some time; it's not visible in daylight.'

We watched this new light drift above for a time until it slipped into the shadow of Orcan. 'It's definitely a ship,' I said. 'A Pitsing great big one.'

Our initial fear was that it was the Empire, back with a second planet cracker; then that it was the despised Commissioner with his reparation goodies. It circled through the night sky – and probably unseen through the daylight hours as well – for two days. 'He's sussing us out.'

'Better put your scythe away, Jorky: he'll have you marked as a trouble-causer.'

The newcomer came down in a shuttle. Settled in the market square. The occupants came out and wandered among us as guests. We showed them round. Stayed polite. They weren't Empire. So they were made welcome, all five of them, officer-crew or whatever.

They wore name patches, not uniforms. Had names like Halberr, Vencci, Aiden.

They had come with an offer that was vastly too good to refuse. A new planet, fresh and fertile, not teeming with an over-abundance of life, but plenty enough. Showed us planetary data, statistics, orbital holos. Every moment of it was a marvel to the folk of Paladas. We were awed by videographs and ground-level holograms, and the offer to take any and all who were willing to go. It was a long way. Out the Empire completely. But the visitor called Halberr Blissen said they had a new propulsion method that would get them there within deccas. His three conditions were that each person signed a document accepting that the new planet – whatever they wanted to call it – belonged to him. It *did* belong to him: he had the purchase papers and crysts to prove it, and he showed them to any of us who wanted to see them. And that each person would pay a once-only lifetime landing fee of one standard unit, whatever their currency was, for living on Blissen's planet; non-returnable, and non-revocable by Blissen. And three, 'You have to renounce all loyalty to the Empire.'

Suspicious of Blissen's offer, Orcan's citizenry demanded all kinds of proof and evidence and details. But Blissen only added that he *did* own the planet, and he wanted it to be occupied by a viable population in the near future, or he might forfeit his rights to it. All internal control of the planet would be ours. Control of defence and off-planet movement would be his responsibility, paid for by a levy on interplanetary trade that he could and would establish. 'We're populating thirty-seven habitable planets in the Wisp – perfectly viable as a closed market cluster. 'I care not who occupies each planet, as long as they're anti-Empire, the more fervently so, the better,' he said. Several times.

'We'll return; right after your harvest next year.' The shuttle left. And the giant ship left. We had about two hundred days, and three of Blissen's representatives remained behind to answer questions, to advise on what could be taken, and to help with any organisation should we decide in favour of moving.

Above all, it was Blissen's requirement of anti-Imperial feeling that swung the population, not the spate of tremors, nor the renewed clouds of gas and steam, nor the bubbling mud and ash lakes, nor even Rheagaea's blessing. Within one hundred days, it was decided that everyone would go. One couple had a romantic vision of staying, and sitting hand-in-hand in red sunsets as Orcan lapsed into fiery splendour around them. However, the Spokesman and his committee decided that they could not let it happen, so their decision was not permitted.

The Orcans never elected a second *Governor*: The post was held in such disrepute, with its links to the Empire, although the name of Dee-ast Gloo was highly honoured. 'He has no doubt become a foot-servant of Rheagaea in the Feast-house of the Gaeans,' Mar-aijja told me.

When Blissen returned, the planet was waiting for him, packed and ready.

Rheagaea! Total wonder when we rose on the ground-to-orbit shuttle, and I saw their craft. Face to face. A tanker. Enormous. It was *vast*. I mean – I'd seen battlecruisers and ten-weights in the past, but this dwarfed them all.

And perched on top was this little yacht. 'Black Angel,' one of the crew said. 'See the magno-clamps and grapples keeping them together? It's the power source – Pitsofalot faster than anything else alive. And its field envelops both craft.'

I stared, mouth pathetically wide open, at everything in sight. I was in orbit for the first time in ten years. 'Yipps, Mar-aijja, just look at the huge size of everything! The organisation, the shuttles and landing lifts, the converted tanker; the numbers of people being moved so quickly and efficiently; the amount of equipment we can take with us – all performed by so few crew. Jeemo!' I marvelled with the inside knowledge of these things. Mar-aijja and Farfallina simply marvelled.

For me, Haiku Sondor Raydd, erstwhile Essny Navigation Officer, it was an Old World resurrected. A whole New Old World – *Pitfire! I'm In Space again.* It had never occurred to me that I ever would be again. It hit me – I ached to be part of it – space, star-travel, plotting vectoral trajectories, a vast ship, shuttles and lifts, machinery, uniforms, organisation, precision.

Throughout my years on Orcan, I'd never missed it, but I was suddenly ripe to experience it all again.

Moving away from Orcan was a huge wrench for me. For almost all the others, it was a tear-filled community wail. A few were glad to see it shrink and vanish, those who'd hated what it had become. But, once we'd gone, the days became long and featureless. I was restless, *There must be so much going on, and I'm not part of it.*

I began to trespass higher up in the converted tanker, the spaces where some of Blissen's landing personnel had quarters, and the Black Angel crew came for recreation, using a single airtube that snaked from one vessel to the other, airlock to airlock, allowing access for personnel. I sought them out when I went visiting. I picked their minds, probed at everything I could think of. Chattered and yarned. Some things, I believed. Much, I disbelieved, especially when they talked about speeds and distances. But I learned fast.

***

Three other communities were aboard, in semi-separated sections of the enormous interior. It was formerly a bulk freight-tanker with vast echoing storage holds, but now it was partly divided into open floors the size of the fields on Orcan, hundreds of them. Each community looked after itself, fed itself.

At one point, the ship took up an orbit, and one of the other communities was disgorged. I never saw the planet or knew its name, but two Orcan young men had debarked with the pioneers, enamoured of two girls. And eight of their youngsters had remained with us.

By sheer persistence and chat-up smarmery, I managed to gain a place at a viewport when the next stop-off was reached, and I watched around seven thousand people being shipped down to a blue and white pearl hanging in the inky blackness; a watery planet, island-strewn, soon to be an idyll to the people who had left behind a planet devastated by Empire forces. They were sad to be leaving the security of the ship, but glad to be arriving. Eleven deccas they had been on the ship, and it had been enough for them.

It was astounding, the numbers going down. Lifts and shuttles constantly moving, carrying hundreds of people, tons of equipment at a time. Planets were being seeded with populations overnight, though Pits alone knew how they would manage once they were left alone.

We had only brought food for eighty days travel, and another eight deccas once we were down. We *needed* to be self-sufficient after that. It was the chance we'd been willing to take.

'Stores, hunting, gathering and fishing until the first harvest,' Spokesman iterated every time fears of the future reared their unknowable head.

After that first period at the view port, I was able to return daily, and I took Mar-aijja and Far-Kijja with me once. They didn't like the grey nothingness when we were moving, nor the starry blackness when the vessel stopped to check directions. We were within The Wisp, in the vicinity of the planets the crew wanted, but it was a matter of locating the right one precisely, and they couldn't easily do that, with their new propulsion and navigation systems, and the sheer momentum and mass of the tanker and its contents. My two ladies were afraid of the gleaming, soulless starpoints of hard light that I was so entranced with. I saw it all in sine curves and apogee points; or beacon locators and 3D directionalism.

Mar-aijja didn't understand my talk of red shift, light years, blue giants, vectors and power orbits, and neither of them would go again. It wasn't like we fell out about it: it was simply that the whole idea frightened them. It scared me, too, when I thought about the reality of the Big Nothing around us.

'How does a clod know about astro-navigation?' came a voice from behind me.

'I've not been a clod all my life,' I turned to see who had spoken. Halberr Blissen. A shorter man than me, eyes that were tired and sparkling at the same time; eyes that danced and laughed and penetrated, and were hard as well as crinkled. I knew him, had seen him on Orcan. But I'd avoided him, one of the first five visitors we'd had. I'd preferred to let the original inhabitants decide their own future when he came calling. I kept off the committee, avoided the meetings, and kept my council to myself. All through that consultation time, I'd been desperate for us to go, but unwilling to influence them, or make them feel obliged to go.

'Come. Tell me,' invited Blissen.

We talked, long and detailed. Among all the sociable chatter, I felt analysed and disassembled by the time Blissen sat back. It was so obvious I was being probed for a purpose: Blissen had sought me out deliberately. Maybe he knew something of my nefarious past, so I decided to be completely open about it, not wanting to be caught out. Plus, I didn't feel the need to hide anything from him.

'Does your wife know all this?' He asked.

I remember feeling guilty when I admitted not.

'Tell her. Then talk to her about coming to work for... *with*, me,' he corrected himself. '*Both* of your ladies.'

Trepidation didn't come into it. I went to speak with them, knowing I had to drain my guilt banks. 'I'll do whatever you want. You're the most important part of my life.'

Mar-aijja knew much of it already, but I started telling them about them of my post as First Navigator of the Red Jacket, in the Empire Space Navy.

'Oh, how wonderful, you were an *officer*!' exclaimed Farfallina.

'In Essny,' reminded Mar-aijja. She knew the jargon already. 'That's where your special cap's from, isn't it, Haik?'

I was surprised how hard it was to talk about the loss of the destroyer Solly Gimlet that went into a black dot, in formation, and didn't come out again.

'Black dot? Is that like a black hole only smaller? Well, everybody knows you don't come out of those.' They were on my side so far.

And I sort-of mentioned murdering seven hundred people on the Fanny F. Flan and the Micron Worlds.

'Well, they were silly names for space ships, anyway,' they agreed.

My role as navigator of the Fly when I visited Goldring came under scrutiny as well. Two Imperial ships had destroyed themselves in that incident, leading to Goldring being destroyed and Orcan being ruined. 'Forgive me,' I said, trembling deep inside.

'Forgive what? For being human? For being you?'

'I wish I'd been there. I'd have done the same.' Farfallina was definitely up for it.

'There's nothing to forgive... silly.' And they were both hugging and kissing me and crying and saying how marvellous I was and how much they loved me and how they never knew I was quite so wonderful, and what a breath-taking new side to my character they saw now. 'You are so kush-vee. Been with you all these years, and we never knew all of that, and *five* Empire ships, and oh, that's wonderful, five... *five*... I bet nobody else *ever* spiked five. And all on your own, too.'

'It's a job. Blissen's offered me a job. I'm not sure doing what.' I was overwhelmed by their response.

'Take it, take it.'

'Yes, you must. I wonder what it'll be. Navigating, do you think?'

'I dunno. More than that, I believe, from what he was saying. It's like we have a bond. I like him, perhaps understand him. Sounds like we had similar experiences with the Empire.'

I felt lame, saying it. 'But what about you... both of you?' I could hardly keep my tears down. 'Our new life on New Orcan?'

'Anywhere, with you. It'll be so exciting. As long as I don't have to look out those window things. I might even get used to the travelling.' Mar-aijja was beaming, eyes a-gleam.

Farfallina was nodding. I took her hand, 'And you, my butterfly? What do you think?' The face of beauty personified in a sad fairy. She couldn't speak: she was too full with the unexpected impact of all his news. Tears filled her eyes and flowed, poured, as she looked at him and still couldn't speak. Fruggit, I was devastated... bewildered. 'What? My love? What? What is it?'

'It hasn't... nothing to do with me.' She struggled the words out through the floods.

I was crying as well. Sheer reaction to her emotion. 'Nothing to do with you? What d... do you mean?'

'It's Mar-aijja... your... wife... who says. And I'm not your wife.' She was standing and turning, but I had hold of her; restrained her, hugging her and telling her, and oh how the pits could I have been so stupid.

'I love you so much. And Mar-aijja. I think of you the same.' And we wept together for a long time, happier through the welter of tears, draining dark holes of fears and secrets that I never suspected existed.

'I'm sorry… sorry.' I kissed and hugged her and we stayed together for long hours. Blissen could wait for his answer. We went to find Spokesman, and were married on the spot. Then it was a quiet supper together with the children and talking about it all. We decided that, as a new and "proper" family, we would find out more about the job, together, before jointly accepting or rejecting it, whatever it was. Mostly, we simply wanted to know more about it first.

'We'll go anywhere, together…'

'It must be better than Orcan, the old Orcan.'

'Turn it down? The way you've been lately? Like a spring crassy-bird with four heads ever since you set foot on this contraption. Impossible.'

'Let's tell him, Yes, whatever.'

'Five Empire ships? Wow, dad, can you prove it? Piddy'll never believe me.'

'I must go and tell Mar-paen and Dar-pmat.'

'I'm not proud of it,' I mumbled after them.

Mar-aijja gazed at me with those wonderful wise beautiful eyes, so penetrating, knowing everything there was to know about me. I felt as though I didn't know anything about her wonderful depths. 'We'll tell him. Yes. Whatever,' she said, so proud, smiling through the little tears that she kept blinking back.

Shell-shocked, I went to see Blissen, with my *wives*.

***

Never, looking round to see what Kopa and Second were up to, have I ever had a single tinge of regret, not at forsaking the promised settled life on New Orcan, nor at joining Blissen's personal staff. As far as I know, the two Mrs. Raydds don't have any regrets either.

Not even now, looking around the green-lit control room of this converted antique battlewagon, crewed by misfits and – now – a barbarian cur. How else could I ever have travelled faster and further than any human has before? Shuggit – It must be the pioneer spirit filling me, even at my age, and with everything I've seen and done.

I suppose, if this is it, I've had a damn sight better and longer life than I could ever have dreamed; more than anyone else I ever heard of – except Hal Blissen, perhaps.

I've become Blissen's confidant, a multi-role trouble-shooter, being sent wherever intuition, experience and reliability are most needed. I couldn't have dreamed of anything like this. Yet here I am, Navigation Officer on a land-based battlewagon that's been outfitted for vacuum survival – and now with a half-understood matter-transmitter being tested under mobile conditions. Actually, a matter transmitter that suddenly turns out to double as a propulsion unit.

I've even piloted and navigated the Black Angel myself on many occasions. I worked on the homing system for the big i/o unit on Discovery, testing the static and moving variances. I've controlled it, and been transported through it more times than I recall. I personally despatched the junk that tore apart the first Empire ship to try to cross the Rift and enter the Wisp. So that makes my tally six, although I can't actually prove it. And I don't want to – all those deaths aren't truly something I would ever congratulate myself about.

Peripherally, I organised the initial population of four planets, and helped to consolidate the Wisp's United Planetary Trading Agency – U.P.T.A. – *The Agency*.

And I'm proud of every single thing I've ever done with Blissen, for Mar-aijja, for F'lina, for the New Orcans, for the populations of the other planets. For the whole Wisp. I became part of the drive that plucked starving populations from their Empire-wrecked homes, and showed them a chance for the future. I believe in all of that. Totally. Blissen is God.

And, right now, I'll kill any of the crew who threatens King's life. An out-Wisp primitive this creature might be, but the memo-melding hasn't destroyed his mind. Our import-accident understands the Unit. If he's going down, it'll be on Blissen's altar. No-one else's.

Thanks to Blissen, I've travelled half the galaxy – koh, maybe not that much. I'm aged one hundred and seventy-five, living and working in the Wisp for a hundred and twenty-five of those years. Mar-aijja's a hundred and forty-some, and F'lina ten years younger than that. We all look fit and fresh; the ladies are mature, yes, but still lovely in face and body and spirit.

No... with his knowledge, the barbarian's invaluable to Blissen, and thus to the Wisp. He's as safe as I can make him.

***

Gazing across at the two crew members – Kav and Stef – with their backs to me, I was recalling a few of the dozens of crew going back fifty years – Watson, Overd, Crigidd, a selection of Sarrits – most of them looking very much like Chix and Vitl – under-sized and black-haired. Stefobeah's different, though – first woman. Unique talents for absorbing all kinds of skills from a memocryst, and harder than plascrete. Her short spells breathing under water had been life-saving on occasion.

Blissen'll be perried about losing Doc and Crossy, though.

I scratched at my stubble hair – all this was making my head itch. My scalp was replaced in an Agency special unit on New Sarrit years ago. But I'm still known as Haiku, or Haik to the crew. Right from when Blissen first asked what I was called, when we went to see him to accept the job. I'd automatically said, 'Haiku', and hadn't had the chance to correct it to Sondor, so it had stuck.

No regrets, not about anything. The whole system works well. Some parts might be hard – like outliving my dozens of children, and multitudinous grandchildren and great-grandchildren. I'm little more than a myth to most of them, a sort of roving senile family friend called Uncle Sondor. Someone of unknown origin, whose job's whispered about.

Yes, some parts are hard, but it doesn't make them any less necessary or right. Like this King primitive. Pitsalone knows how he'll do it, looking at Hilda's co-ordinate figures, but he *will* do it. I'll make damn sure he will, because, without him, I'll never return to Mar-aijja and F'lina again. And that's not going to happen.

Well, the whole intention of this foray was to explore the i/o unit in a mobile setting. So we've been totally successful. Except, I suppose, Blissen wanted Doc and Crossy to come and tell him all the details. Can't blame the barbarian for that, I suppose.

So now, I have to protect King; convince the crew we'll be safe if we return to the Wisp; persuade or force King to operate the unit – a bit like making the condemned man pilot the flybug to the gibbet cross.

But, if he doesn't know...

Let's see if he's conscious...

Down the spiral: three crew were in the i/o room. To the left, the hairy-barian was laid out on his bunk in the crew-room, twitching and mumbling.

'King?' I pushed at him.

He stirred, rolled to look up. Struggling to focus, sitting up and reaching for the glass lenses to fit on his face, 'Mmm?'

'Are you up to speaking – private? You understand private? You and me?'

'About?' Distrust personified on that animal-hairy face.

'What you want, or need... Different clothes? Clean ones. Food? drink? Getting you somewhere safe? Medic attention?'

The look on him – silent and suspicious. He smoothed his facial hair with both hands, and adjusted his eye-lenses slightly with a fingertip. 'What do you want?'

His accent was enough to make me wince. But I hadn't expected more than a grunt or face-pull of bafflement. 'I think we can help each other.'

'Get me back? You wrecked my Austin Healey. I had things to do. I was going to— Jeez I hurt.'

'Yes, yes, we can help you. But first, *we* need to return where we came from—'

'No, you don't: spaceship was about to fire at you, at us. Everybody tell me. Pack of maniacs y'are.' He was almost falling aside. Eyes glazing over.

'Ah, yes... yes. We can fix you. The original transfer – getting you here – was accidental. Physically, it didn't quite import you, er, in tune. A fraction out of phase. You seem to be recovering, slowly. When we get back, we can treat you, help you. You could get us there?'

'Christ, I can't stop shaking.'

'King. King. Concentrate, you know how the unit works, don't you?'

'I… I did. I dunno.' One sagging breath. 'Send me back. Need to be on Earth. Or kill me off. Jeez, I feel awful.'

'Yes, of course,' I lie so easily. 'We can get you back. No problem. Just need this doing first. Then get you well, hmm?'

Pit-born was staring up at me, swathed in disbelief. *Fruggit. You know we can't operate the unit… can't get you home.*

Ease back. Get some trust. You're not stupid, are you? You understand the i/o unit – and probably the situation we're in. Will you believe any reassurances?

Another twenty careful minins with him, and the only upside I could think of was that I was still alive, and that was as much as I'd hoped for on more than a few of the past fifty-thousand-odd days skipping the spaceways.

Vastly overweighing that single positive, the downside was that the solution to the i/o unit's operation might, or might not, be lurking in the scrambled and de-phased brain of a near-dead, disbelieving primitive.

Right, my barbarian friend-to-be, I need you to trust me enough to work with me to understand the i/o cylinder as a drive unit, work out how to control it, and find out precisely where we are

Then plot a 3D vector route to get us back to the Wisp – where you just rescued us from the talons of death. So that involves convincing you how much better things will be for you when we get there.

Just keeping you alive's not going to be easy: if the out-of-phase disruption to your body and brain doesn't kill you, I expect the crew'll still be wanting to airlock you.

Oh, shuggs… scrubbing at my scalp, I stared into the barbarian's near-blank eyes. *On every level of thinking, this is impossible… hopeless.*

Hi ho… I'd best warn Kopa we don't stand a chance.

Up the spiral stairs I weary went, sparked myself up for the last couple of steps, whispered a couple of prayer-words to Rheagaea, and crossed my fingers.

'Commander, I got it all figured out. We're going to be just fine.'

I WAS JUST COMING TO THAT

'Doze! Daisy Doze!'

Half-way across the transit lounge, three-thou kee above Central City, I stopped.

Like, when you're called Daisy Doze, the last thing you want is having your name shouted out in public. Which is entirely down to my mother having a heavy cold when she took me to be named. 'You should have been Maisie Rose,' she always insisted, 'But it's done now, and I'm not taking you back to change it.'

But here I am, fresh – or not so fresh after 38 days solid on the trip from Entira, by way of a couple of scrubby pass-me-by planets that I vowed never to go within a light-day of, ever again. All I wanted was to get my gravity legs back, via a visit to a thousand bars down in CC.

I turned. It was Eski Dost! Hey – My old friend from Gamze. His voice had changed: that's usually because of radiation and vac exposure when it gets like that. And he was a genuine old friend, not the type who just think they are, or want to be. We hugged and shared a pout-peck and he stared at my chest like he always did, lustful old herrif. We really had to park in the lounge bar for a catch-up drink or two; and probably a good bit more, besides. We're like that – really good friends.

'So where've *you* been, Dais?' when he calmed down from giving me the news from back home, and the rest of the universe.

'Well... I was doing routine trading runs around the IR 78 circuit for a while. As interstell routeways go, it isn't heavily used—'

'Hardly used at all, from what I hear, not till lately, anyway.'

'It wasn't used much at all, back then,' I said, 'although it's been a right of way since the Year Zero. But that new colony planet called Zoozun kept putting obstructions in the way – necessitating diversions, causing crashes – electro beams, pirates, knocked out the part-way beacons. The Fed refused to listen to complaints. They just used to send standard replies—'

'I bet they kept saying that Zooti, the parent planet of the colony, is a prominent member of the Federation?' Eski knew the Fed's standard brushoff to any complaints, 'Yeah, we had them a couple of times, out Revell way.'

'But it was the direct route between Zylaz and—'

'Madrihenath.'

'Interrupt me once more, Eski, and bed's off.' I gave him the deep stare. He took the hint, pushed his mouth shut with a fingertip. Bed with me is a prospect not to be lightly spurned. 'Remember it, Eski – butt in once more, and you're sleeping alone tonight. Okay?

'Right,' I carried on, 'I was subbing with some old-Cap out of Procee. Name of Gilbert Sull—' Eski stifled his interruption in the nick of bedtime. 'We had to give up travelling that way after the Zoozuns mounted a disruptor on Farway Beacon. It screwed our engine to Mordo and back, and the re-phasing on the Mark Two was too expensive to have it fixed out the petty coinage. So, while Capn Gil expected to be out of action long-term arranging loans and back-vac repairs, I ended up on local delivs, people, goods, any stuff. Pretty much had to work my way back up again with whoever needed a flight officer.

'But I have qualiffs by the console-full and got hired as cap by EZee Fraiting Inc, based on Faller – risky loads to dodgy destinations, all borderline freighting; high risk – like of explosions, creature escapes, chemical and radiation leaks, pirates, customs, rivals. But we were well-armed. EZee was good that way – a vhp ruptor gun with auto-guide systems.' I paused to give Eski a chance.

'You don't keep records of all that? It's deep no-no stuff.'

'Records? You jest – it was highly illegal on most planets to even know what some of the things were. Then one time, we were smuggling a massive arms shipment plus general supplies to Modrig, where there was a rebellion. But Faller home gov was suddenly deciding to clamp down – enforcing a complete embargo on the whole System. So we were told to hold off.

'It turned out someone had snitched on the whole setup. Fed agents were all over EZee, and we had a panic call to cover up, get out, get rid; anything but be caught with a cargo like that. It was irridinium – enough to blow half a planet back to primal dust. "We don't care what you do with it. Just get rid of it," they told us—'

'That'd be about the time Zoozun was smithereened, wasn't it?' Eski simply couldn't resist butting in.

'Well—'

'Damn planet was totally disintegrated, I heard?'

'Well, if you'll just—'

'They never did get to the bottom of it, did they?' Eager Eski at it again.

'*Shut up, Eski!* Zoozun? The terrible, inexplicable obliteration of that poor fledgling planet? I was just coming to that. And what did I say about not interrupting?'

DON'T ASK

A drink appeared in front of me. Tall, pink, gracile lines – very attractive. She was, too. I gazed up at her. Bit blurred. I always get smash-brained the day before a long trip. Not incredible-long, you know. Well, it is. If one hundred-thirty days is long by your reckoning. I get smash-brained, and find a few people to hate and have a brush with. Then I can spend the first ten days recovering, and the rest of the time glad I'm well away from them. So it helps.

This creature can go away, I'm thinking. It's bother I want. Not some delicate flower of womanhood who's looking for a bit of rough.

She's probably a clone – too much my dream skag. Some yucker's been picking at my head again to create this vision especially to entrap me.

She wants a ride to Keffaldm. On my ship. No skagging chance. 'Foff,' I told her.

Would she chuffaslike be told no.

Told her. 'I do on-my-own, not pairings. Foff.'

She was desperate. Said she was. Didn't look it. Looked dreamy. Thus a non-reality. 'Foff,' I repeated.

Bringing me drink after drink, she was getting me brashed out my lolly, off my dolly and up the Molly Perdinz. Who's going to resist that? Not a real man, i.e, one who's locking himself in a tin tube for the next four cycles. No contest – endless ooze and the smartest tart that ever lurked in my head – my resistance was brilliant. I was telling her, 'I don't take passengers – they're a liabil-something. All of'em. Male, female, or Yi'opps from Yeston. I've heard of too many of them skagging-up the journey – for good.'

I hear rumours of how passengers attempt to sabotage the drive, skag-up the navvy system, double-open the airlock, overload the String unit – now that's caused some spectacular blow-ups. Spectacular, if anybody had witnessed them, that is. The log signals come drifting in on some beacon years later.

'I only ever take eight passengers anywhere, max. And I've only been doing that since I got the Neck'n'Do system. They never like it, course. But I insist they wear it, in case they go batty. The neckie? Why? I needed something of that nature out there. Get all sorts of toonies in the Big Black. Goes to their vac, as the saying goes.

'On take-off, you have to be in an acceleration cocoon. The rest of the trip you have to wear a neckie – which guarantees you behave.'

She looked more dubious with every word I spoke.

'How you going to pay for a trip like that?' I asked her. 'It's beyond price. You can't buy it. So how y' going to pay?'

'What do you want, my body?'

I looked her up and down. 'Yes. That'd be very nice, thank you. But I let you aboard, then you change your mind – so what do I do? Tie you to the B deck bulkhead and have my wonderful way with you for one-thirty days? Hardly. Or cut my losses and give you a one-way tour of the airlock? Not my style. But, if you wear a neckie, you do exactly what I tell you. Hmm?

That stilled her up.

'It was you who offered,' I pointed out. 'No obligation. You know where the exit is – right where you came in.'

So she stands there, all prim and pretty and biting her lip.

'Once a day, no more.' She made the initial offer.

Ah, you're into negotiating the details, are you? I bet your nipples are the same flushed pink as your face.

'Minimum. I might feel especially skaggy some days.'

From what little I can see of you, that might well happen.

'And if I don't... feel especially... er?'

'Doesn't matter. You do it anyway. It's not that I blow your head off. You just do what I tell you. It's automaton-like when you're wearing a neckie. Wanna try it? Sample each other?' I offered her the neckie I always carry.

After a few more slops of the ooze, she slipped it round her neck, locket at her sternal notch. 'Just there,' I touched the base of the throat. 'Yes. Right. Now whistle me outa here.'

'What!? You mean?'

'Yep. What did you expect? Kneel down.'

'Here? No! In a bar? Give you a spout pout?'

'Yep. Get on with it while I finish both our drinks.' The look on her face! Don't think she'd done it before, but must have known what it meant, cos after a moment or two of me thinking it at her – kind of giving her the mental picture, not too pressured or intense, she knelt down between my knees, and was the star of the Equinock's Arms.

It's just a total compulsion you feel. You have to do what they say. No two ways about it. It's not a choice of doing, or getting a blinding headache that tends to be fatal if allowed to continue. No – you do it. Can't help it.

Yes, enjoyed that. Took the neckie off her. 'Thank you very much, Yaylene. Now get yourself back to wherever, hmm?'

She swayed; somewhat groggy when she stood.

'You've been good... very good.' I congratulated her, thanked her and removed the neckie.

She looked more than somewhat abashed. Hadn't wanted to do it. But she had to know what wearing a neckie meant. 'Now chuffalong.' I watched her totter away, lesson learned. Pity, really. She was cloned from my dreams. *Mmm, the body she's hiding under there.*

Okay, so... once she'd wobbled off, it didn't matter where I crashed now. I knew I'd wake up sometime, and wend my staggery way down to the V4 bay in the docks, and push the button. One hundred thirty days thereafter, I'd be settling into orbit round Keffaldm, wanting another cargo, preferably one that took me swiftly out of the most isolated planetary garbage heap in existence. I mean whoever heard of Keffaldm? Jeeks – it's a pit – I been once before. One of the most on-its-own-and-no-wonder planets there could be. And that silly buffer had wanted to go there. What the fluffing foo for?

So it was sometime later I woke up. Sort of. Bleared half-awake, more like. Sheeks, the room crashed in and out my mind and my vision, and I knew I got to get down to V4, so I tried to shake the weight off me. And shove it off, and looked what was crushing me down, tentacles all over me... Skag me backwards. *Her,* draped all over me. Not letting go. Not tentacles – just a long slim arm, with fingers like the giffs of Macker Lew, inside my shirt and tensing slightly on my chest. Nice as that felt, I had to ease her away, crawl to my feet, sway a mite, get up again... three or four times, and leave the little angel-pot lying there.

'Didn't think you could lose me that easily, did you?' She caught up with me at the door, where I was getting accustomed to the awful brightness of the high UV light on Violetta before stepping out into it. I say stepping, but it was more like overbalancing.

Insisted on staying with me all the way down Main and Klin's to the Shuttle-Up, wheedled her way on the next sicky-lift up to orbit and wouldn't let go till she was asking me how the airlock closure mechanism worked.

'You have to wait a mome. It'll seal us in, full auto, measure our masses, adjust the settings and costings—'

'Costings?'

'Sure. What do you weigh? On a planet like Vio? Two-fifty-ish? So that's around a millionth of the weight of this ship. You want us to pull up half a lightyear short of Keffaldm cos it didn't factor us in on the fuel, settings, and parabolas? Everything has to be absorbed and accounted for; there needs to be a millionth more fuel, for emergencies – not that any are survivable in space, but a half percent margin for external factors... You know the sort of thing.

'Now then,' I tried to turn round and tell her – 'Ooooh... not too quick or I'll fall over... get that neckie collar on... where the foogle is it?' Rooting in my pockets... 'never mind, got three spare in the cab locker.

'Here,' she's already put it on, locket nestled in her sternal notch – snugged in there a treat. Phew... looked good there. Time to give her a trial run before we departed? Maybe... shuggs, no, not really; not something to be rushed, first time with someone. Specially at the start of a four-cycle lock-in.

Wondered what I'd let myself in for when I slipped her into the cocoon for launch. So divinely neat lying there. Looked kinda fearful-trusting-untrusting-but-gotta-do-it. Slid myself into the vomit-bag next to her – I usually puke up after a heavy five-dayer and an acceleration burst like we were in for. Could see her there, alongside me… two more unused cocs beyond her, for occasional passenger runs. And six more in the cubby hold.

So I taps the live pad and wait for ten – no reason, I just do it. Then touch again for Go – and blanked out as the power kicked in.

It's usually a few days later that I come round – initial acceleration over, main sequence to watch, and send the Visual Verify back to base – not that they could do anything. They just like to know. She – Yaylene – was already awake, but stuck in her pod and frantic. So I let her out and told her that she owed me for three days unused sex quota and she tried to get the neckie off and of course it is un-get-offable.

***

'Right? So that, basically, is the story of how me and your mother met. Now, are you gonna take this neckie off me?

'You want to know what? I only agreed to answer one question, not one from each of you.' I looked along the line – the Eight Wonders of the Universe, I call them.

'Oh, alright then… Yes, Sidkin, my treasure, you were born not too long after that trip out to Keffaldm.

'Tylee? What? Have I? No – *never*, not like you mean, anyway…

'Joey? What's your question? Ahh, I was hoping you wouldn't ask about *that…*'

COUPLA YUMANS

Bristling his feelers and tentacle-tips, Jasper was becoming irate at the ET Vets, 'They're running a yonk behind time,' he complained to the pair of three-toed lemmikits by his side. 'No wonder, with all these furricking câini that folk bring in. They don't look after'em. Get all sorts of diseases and injuries – no control over them, and no love for'em. Just status pets. Huh! Câini! As much status as a crock o'dildos in my book. Come on, you two, safer round this side in case they break loose, eh?' He patted his left side, and they relievedly sidled round, complete with safety harnesses and years of loving training and companionship. Settling better now they were less visible to the quadsome of snarling, yapping câini down the far end.

'These folk bring'em in… no control over'em. Wouldn't be the first time one got free in here,' he underbreathed into his backup lungs. 'Just hark at all their rattle. Probably in for injections to keep up their sterilisation programme. They could do with calming jabs, too. Why can't they behave like you two, eh, *miaj amiki?'*

Giving his lemmikit companions another loving stroke and scratch on their wing casings, he looked around. 'There's a couple more lemmikits across there, see? You want to go and chat? No? Not bothered? Okay. Be grateful you're not down the end there, eh?'

They looked again at the rowdy câini in the corner, all twisted fascias and painted palps. 'We'll stick with you gorgeous pair, eh, Joey? And maybe an occasional aivy, eh, Chloe? Look at them two just coming out the consulting room, them and their beaks, eh?' Jasper grinned at his companions, mimicking the avians' classical pecking movements. 'Ho! Look who's just waddled in – Uncle Freedman – you remember him? Yes, last Founder's Day at his place. Those lemmimiskins you got on so well with, eh? And all the presents and drinks and nibbles, hmm? And Doily Dolly putting on that show. You do recall that, huh?'

Waiting for his friend to finish booking in at the reception, Jasper called as he turned, 'Ay up, Freedy, what you got there?'

Waving and smiling with both faces, Freedman seated himself a respectful distance along the bench, carefully putting a sturdy carry-case on the floor. 'Hi, Jazzer. In here? Coupla yumans that Conro's had for some time – a breeding pair at the end of their term. He was going to send them back, as per contract, but they filled in the application forms to stay on. Conro din't want to keep'em any longer, so I took'em off his feelers.'

Jasper slid along to sit next to the newcomer. 'Yumans, eh? They want to be re-adopted, hmm? Let's have a look; I an't seen any before.' He peered into the smart porta-box. 'Funny looking things, aren't they? Got their bones inside, I hear? Can I poke one? Never felt one before…'

'Sure, they don't mind.' Freedy slid the housing box closer. 'Just take it slow at first – they're kinda nervous till they realise y' not going to rip'em in half or something. They're quite tough. "Resilient, amiable and amenable" as the adverts used to go.'

Jasper reached into the container and waited a moment, then felt around… 'Yoik! Soft, innit? They seem fine, but I hear some folks have been dumping them? Like tossing them out the hover in the scrublands, into the river, or feed'em to the câini?'

'Yeah, it's been happening – not so much these days.' He dropped a tentacle into the carry-box to give reassurance to his two yumans.

'So what they been doing with Conro?'

'Breeding, mostly. That's why I'm here – give'em a check-up. They've had twenty-five live births in five years – a crop of five a year. I want to make sure they're alright before I take them on.'

'What for? Conro wanting to sell'em on?'

'He was, but buying and selling yumans ain't allowed any more, especially when they're free of contract. There was a dark-market for'em till about four years ago. Then they found the offspring of the super-induced and radiated ones didn't thrive – took a lot longer to mature, and 50% death rate before maturity. So contracts, imports and sales dried up. Like you said, some yumans were discarded – dropped out the transports well out of town and left to fend for themselves – kitts and all.'

Jasper was almost sorry for the poor little things looking up at him out their box. 'So they're free now, out of their contracts?'

'Yeahhh. They weren't happy, either. Nowhere to go; no real niche for them here, not on their own.' Freedy gave one a comforting hug with a spare tendril.

'But Conro kept'em till end of?'

'Yeah, soft, he is. He quite liked having'em round – unusual sort of decoration to have in the house and garden. Like tentacle-candy. But, and it's a big *but*, he's got himself paired-up with that lassie from Dexter. You know the one? All proboscis, eye stalks and "I've got ten minutes to spare, Sonny-boy" when it suits her.'

'From Dexter? What's the problem with that?

'Quite a few of them are addicted to raising a particular breed of câini, called pibuqa. She's got four of'em. Trouble is, they attack yumans on sight. I remember a few fight matches at one time. Very popular, too. But illegal even then. Gov'ment clamped down on it.'

'Oh? Yumans getting wiped out, were they?' Jasper gazed at the pair of strange aliens in the box.

'Mostly not – they learn fast, out-organised the pibuqa, out-fought'em. It was the Câini Authority on Dexter that put pressure on to stop it.'

'So, what you gonna do with these two? Breed? Or have'em neutered while you're here?'

'Not absolutely sure with this pair – they got a lot of kitts already and seem pretty stretched, even with all the help. Conro was ultra-fertilising them, so without that, they'd probably be down to one a year at most. Which would be fine for what we're thinking of.'

'So what you got in mind, Freedy?'

'Well, I already keep a few at home. In the house to start with, then move'em into the pen.'

'Pen?'

'Yeah, like a little compound; just a cluster of yuman-style houses we made specially for them; we get a bit of funding – private and gov.'

'I suppose they'll be like broken-in by the time they get to you, all these private five-year contracts they come in on? Getting them used to life here, us, the language? Must be interesting – for you and them?'

'It's working that way,' Freedy said. 'They pick up the language really quick after the injections and memocrysts. I give'em memo-drops specially tailored to yuman brains… their thinking patterns.'

'How many you got? Cute, aren't they? You always dress'em up like that?'

'No, just for this visit; they got lots of outfits, usually their own choice. After a bit we let them out on their own. They home back – I always have their chips re-programmed so they know where to come, and they do – no coercion. Plenty of freedom. Me and Jaine have more than a hundred adults now, plus five times as many under ten years old. And they seem to be doing fine – slow growth, but not dying off like they used to.'

The ET Vet buzzed for the next one to go through, a pair of snakeshifters from Bryns. Jasper and Freedy watched their holder gather them under his tentacles, and struggle with their collars as they went in.

'You've started your own yuman outpost at that rate, Freedy. What for?'

'Yes, it is like a little colony: "The Village", they call it. For the longer term, we've been in talks with the gov and investors, about using them as puppet colonists for a couple of other planets.'

'No?' This was new thinking to Jasper. 'Puppet colonists? What's one of them? What for?'

'There's this planet called Zeppler – dozen light years away – and another one that's two light years further out. They're both in our sphere, but not habitable for us – there're traces of argon and neon in the atmosphere. So, bearing in mind this is for the medium-long-term—'

'You're going to seed them with these yumans?'

'Already started. We have a village-style base on Zeppler, small and done a lot of support for them, but it's coming on. We did a prelim survey, and they've followed it up in two chosen areas – land they can farm, and mine for building and construction materials. Plus a nice little port on the coast.'

'You been, have you?'

'Not yet. But I'll be taking the first volunteers from my community out there and get them settled. Start of next year. The pioneer groups can't wait to get more settlers in, expand. Big planners, they are.' He smirkled fondly into the carry-box, offered them a warming zolper. 'If it works well, we'll offer it as a package to newcomers, like all the ones who used to come in on the Companion contracts. Give'em one year here on Ekhaya to learn about us, see us as friendly, speak Stang, raise their skills. Their home planet is over-crowded and under-resourced. So this'll help the situation there, too.

'So it's like proxy colonising? What the chuffing chewbits would you be doing that for?'

'A: to stop the kytes moving into that sector from the Out-Fringe Region; B: to create economies we can trade with; that's always mutual benefit. And C: maybe act as early warnings for us if there is bother with the kytes. At the very least they should be friendly towards us if we help'em, set'em up with their own planet and everything. Like I said – long term policy – buffer zone.'

He smirkled affectionately again. 'Besides – D: Jaine and I, we love'em; it's great to have them around. And they know it; they like us.' He reached towards them again. 'Eh? My little chucks?'

SHIMMER

Within, I am so thrilled – for the first time since I became a Shimmer, I'm permitted to take my own decisions. Outside, I show nothing. Because I am nothing, a non-form. I keep mentally hugging myself, and suppressing my excitement. Who would have dreamed it? *Me. I am become a Shimmer.*

Insubstantial now, on this amber beach, I drift along. No, not drifting, *shimmering* along it, I remind myself. The lowering sun sparkles off the unsettled surface of sea, bathing the cubdub trees in a wondrous orange glow.

There's a girl a little further ahead, a human. She's early for the beach party they have planned. Unseen, I sleek towards her, and hover close. Unnoticed, I slide into her body. Ahh… I bathe in her strength and youth. So much like I once was, a few years since. For a moment, I appreciate her body – when I was young, what I would have given for these, the firmness of my breasts. I'm so slender and healthy in here. A momentary joy to be in such a fine young body.

Others are arriving. Youngsters, youths and girls getting a fire started. I observe from within my host for a time as they make their preparations for their evening party between the cubdubs and the sea. Male or female, I slide from one to another, as I've learned to do of late. All unaware of my presence within them, such a change to be doing it in the wild, as it were. Not under supervision in an indoors, more controlled environment.

Oh, my! I know this arm… it was one of mine. I've never re-met one of my own body parts before. How interesting to recognise it, to feel it fitting so naturally into this girl – another fine young woman. Not a twinge along the joining region, though she's energetic, playing a beach high-ball game for a time.

Another fire is being lit further down the beach, just beyond a small group of rocks. My host pauses from the game and looks, and speaks: 'They're not humans. They're dories.'

I remain lodged within the girl as I listen in with them as they look towards the rival beach party, studying the newcomers, 'Dories? You're right. They've come by sea.'

'What have those things come for?' says another girl who joins us.

'I don't like them,' my host is saying, 'half-humans who live mostly in the water. They're not natural, even if we are quasi-kindred.'

'Cross-breeds, more like. Perversions of nature.' A tall youth was pulling faces as he spoke and drank and spat. 'Nothing but trouble between us.'

'Specially when they turn up like this...'

'On our beach...'

'I feel restless, just seeing them. I don't believe I've seen dories so close before... Will they be there all evening? All night?'

'I imagine so.'

'Shouldn't be any bother, not from a couple of hundred paces away. It'd take them best part of a minin to get here on this soft sand. With their physiques, they could probably swim it quicker.'

'Would they do that? Come this way?' My host was more than uneasy, becoming frightened at the prospect of a horde of semi-aliens dashing and flapping towards her, wielding clubs or blades – she couldn't decide which.

'They might. We're open to attack from them if they start acting the way I've heard… Treacherous creatures. Their minds are from the depths, as well as their finny bits.'

I slide into him, wanting to encounter his more focused thinking, *Which way could we run if the dories attack? What might I grab in self-defence? I think I'm in with a good chance with Haylee tonight… beach party… warm… campfire… Haylee in a protect-me mood.*

Most of my host's friends are looking and wishing the dories hadn't come so close… or at all. I slip among them, shimmering unsuspected. I'm better at this than I feared I might be, out here, unsupervised. Several thinking of what there is nearby to use as weapons, perhaps sneak over there, quietly, and attack them before they come on a raid down here.

'Or a racing attack and get them first…'
'We could move further down the other way…'
'Why should we? We were here first.'
'Look at'em, silhouetted there.'
'Yeah, big fire they've built.'
'Yeah,' they laughed, 'Must make a warming change from the bathic depths.'
'Mmm, bring a glow to their finny bits, I bet.'

**

When the Dories' music came on, my then-time host stopped in his poking at the fire and looked down the beach to the other partying group, thinking, *I bet we look the same to them – black shapes against a big campfire, under the cubdub trees, waves lapping. Except we're against a black night sky, and they have the remains of the sunset as their backdrop.*

Looks pretty good like that, my next host is thinking. I detect a twinge of jealousy that we aren't looking like that to anyone, so I decide to give that thought a little extra push. *Wouldn't mind being over there, with that on the platter...*

A well-rounded youth I move into is already wrinkling his nose, *What the Kaori is that smell they're cooking up?* I'll just ease in an extra thought that it smells pretty good. *Mmm, yes,* he's thinking, *smells good.*

I'll take it easy; let them ripen up their worrying and fretting a little more... it'll give me something more specific to work on. It looks as if I have the easier side tonight, even though I'm working alone for the first time. Trusted. Three of my fellow shimmies have infiltered the dories. I can sense them poking the dories along already. The sea-humanics always arrive weaponed-up – tusks and narteeth blades are pretty standard for them. But that's principally defence against shakros in the shallows when they're body-surfing. Yipperty – the time I occupied a dory – under supervision, of course, when I was so new to this. It was a whole new world for me, literally: they're from a planet they call Marra.

Humans – including me before my transformation to Shimmer – have been here much longer. But they're here now, mostly in the seas, a few marshland and estuary colonies, and even a few on drier land – increasingly so...

Gazing towards them, my new host is thinking, *Filthy and disease-ridden.*

- No, no, they're not, I ease in with a touch of doubt, of disbelief.

I heard they smell of fish?
- Not that either...

Bodies like theirs, they must think like cooderfish.
- Only when attacked.

The dory I'd once been in, surfing the waves, was a little darling by human standards, but getting that across to my erstwhile fellow humans is another matter. But it's what I'm here for.

They look like tentacled mud-skippers, you know.
- I suppose they can look like that, sometimes. But they can stand upright, like pingus, and their wing-fins can extend into arms and fingers. They haven't quite mastered the idea of palms and thumbs yet, but they're getting better.

They're cold-blooded in mind and body, my original girl is thinking on my revisit.
- No, neither, actually – they have good body-temp control from a few degrees above freezing to around seventy percent boiling. And they think in the same basic way that human people do, about the same things. They have their loves for each other, and fears of others.

Which is why we Shimmers are here tonight: At this time of year there are often beach parties along here in the evenings. Starting tonight, the sardinyas are running, coming into the shallows, and the humans and dories'll be getting in each other's' way. They'll not be competing, exactly, for the dories fish in the deeper areas, and the humans only as deep as they can wade, or from rocks – being watchful for the prowling shakros.

Perfect circumstances for a battle of beach rivals that would set relations back a generation… and this is the first night of a six-day run of the sardinyas; a practice for the following nights when the other packs of humans and dories will descend along the whole beach. And we don't want bother escalating, do we, with a mass of fire-branches and spear-guns against narteeth blades and coral clubs?

So we hope to forestall any signs of trouble, and let them co-exist. Calm relations between them.

**

My humans are taking some influencing: there's a lot of unease among them – among *us* – I'm one of them tonight. I sense rumours, tales of dark deeds by the fish-folk along the beach. I try to settle my group down, to think in peaceful party mood, slipping unsensed from one to another, spending longer with some than others – the most wary ones, and those who are most open to sociable thinking, to encourage their voices.

Some are thinking the dories look almost human in the firelight. *That music… drifting between us, strange, unworldly tones, but not unpleasant, in fact, quite alluring.* I dart from one to the next, calming them. Jipps – I remember that arm when it was mine. Good'un it was…

Gradually, I'm persuading them down to a quiet beach-night calm, to positivity... bringing inquisitiveness into their minds.

That music reminds me...
And the aroma of that food...
Looks less breezy in the shelter of those rocks...

All totally unaware of my presence among them, within them, though some are wondering about the dories. I prod a little, here and there... curious... positive.

Expecting more resistance from the dories than the humans, three of my fellow Shimmers are within them, quelling fears, relaxing to the mood of the music, smoothing the optimism. Perhaps the dories are wishing the humans would welcome them onto the beach for a change... would perhaps discuss sharing the fishing on the morrow...

But a couple of mine are reaching around for their spear guns; untrusting thoughts niggling at them. I suppress my sharp pang of panic and delve within them, easing their thoughts, pressing, urging their hands towards to their dishes and drinks flasks instead.

'Their cooking sure smells good...'

'Do you suppose we might offer them some drink in exchange?'

'They can't make their own drinks, can they?'

'We could try, I suppose...'

'Why not? We got plenty.'

'And share their shelter?'

'That music reminds me of the time Yoanna and I...'

'They're reckoned to be awesome dancers...'

'Slink and slither like eels on eagerjuice.'

Gradually – so slowly – there was a general movement among my people, reaching for a flask to take, or a hamper to carry, someone's hand to hold in reassurance, as they almost unspeakingly began the two hundred-pace walk to the rocks where the dories danced and sat, cooked their food and played their music.

*

Perhaps if I'm successful here, and the next few projects, Shimmer Council will consider upping me a level next year, and allow me to undertake an assignment *completely* on my own. Who knows? – even to roam and find my own cases of need; possibly to work independently with dories sometimes.

Eventually I could be eligible to work with some of the higher life forms... the Martuyi... the Yabanci. Perhaps even *Cats*.

***

ALL FOR ONE

'You stupid skudding vitch, Bauer Two-Grade.'

Insulting yogger. I looked up.

Bridge Officer Ruyfe towered over me. He'd seemed alright before, in his ivory-white uniform and arctic teeth, when I'd seen him in the briefing hall. It was grey and blue in there, and the uniform had looked pretty smart. But down here in the bright chrome and satin silver engine room, his uniform clashed, and so did he.

Not that we'd had much to do with each other previously, workwise. And certainly not socially. Him being a Bridge-level officer, and me the grease-girl (Second Class) for the Number Three Drive Unit. That's what he told me, anyway.

'The Crawler-in of Narrow Spaces,' as he'd called me, very forcefully a few sentences ago.

Along with 'stupid zitter' and 'skudding bitch'. From an officer!

He went ranting on, spittle flecking all over me. But I had to stand and take it. *It'll wipe away afterwards, and I'm due for a vac-bath at shift-end.* So I let him snarl and shout on. Like I had a choice. Obvious he was trying to provoke a reaction from me. That'd be so he could charge me, and then take sexual advantage on a promise of letting the charge lapse. He even slapped my face! That is just so totally beyond. Officers don't do that. It's a CM offence to strike any member of crew or additional personnel. Except in the case of cowardice when confronting the enemy, naturally. *Must imagine he'll get away with it in here, with only me present – and that was because of a blowback on Number Four Drive Unit that had seriously debilitated all three crew – so they'd had to make up with crew from the other drive units.*

So now he's trying to grab me, 'Come on,' he said. 'It's all for one aboard this ship.'

Maybe, I thought, *but we're not all for you.*

Five mins ago, I'd told him it wasn't me who'd been on duty the shift when he was claiming the incident had occurred. 'I am not responsible, Sir.' I told him once, very clearly. Once should be enough. He's an *Officer* – equals intelligence, sense, manners, leadership and all the other propaganda brain-mush they tell you in Basic.

I would have been distraught – none of this was my fault in any way. But he was marking me down. Leering at me, staking his claim for me to be his gropy this tour. Plus, I'm sensible. Level headed. Calm. I know it will pass and all will be well. I always tell myself that in personal or battle situations. I find it helps.

'I'll show you.' I ducked under his grasping reach, and strode across the drive-room, 'See here... down here in the shaft. This is where the ion particles condense. That indigo tinge means the setting is perfect.'

He looked down the shaft, into the total blackness beyond the indigo. 'That's where the saying comes from, you know, Sir – "Beyond the Indigo"? Okay, Sir? Now,' I ducked again and stepped over to the console, 'put your hand on the pad, you'll see the readouts, the maintenance logs. It will show that I was not present on that shift—'

He hit me again; even put his pocket pad down to free his hand for another go at me.

That was twice too often, and raised him to Vengeance-is-Mine status. There was effall his fellow officers would do if I made a complaint. Impunity was probably his middle name; with Pillock and Gonad before and after.

I twisted away and slipped against the console where we'd been checking the readouts. My fingers landed beside the keypad he'd just left there. So simple to slide it into a pocket. He'd find himself in a bit of a tizzy and tinkle when he realised he'd lost it. Out he stalked, furious, vowing he'd have me laid over an oxy-unit before the trip was out.

Will you, indeed? I watched him go. He'd do it. I'd heard rumours about him. Raping Ruyfe, they called him in Stores.

I fingered his keypad... I was alone in the drive unit of the Engine Room Level. *He'll be back when he realises. Unless he deliberately left it here so he can accuse me of stealing it? Yes, that's a distinct possibility. You got to do something, girl. But what?*

**

Just a matter of being precise, exercising judgement. I steadied myself, and held the little keypad on the edge of the ion shaft. Very carefully, I aimed it so it would slide down the shaft and... ahh, yesss... lodge against one of the injector nozzles at the twenty-carr mark. About a third of the way down.

Right. No time to waste, in case he realised his loss, or came back to accuse me, so... *Do I press the General Alarm? Or...?* I pinged up to Internal Security that there was something in the ion drive unit, down the Number Three shaft. 'Looks like an officer's keypad,' I told them. 'Under no circumstances can the drive be initiated—

'Yes, Sirs, I know it's not up to me to tell you—

'Certainly I'm aware of Battle Amber Status at the moment, yes, Sirs—

'Instant readiness compromised? Well, yes. It would blow the ion drive apart if it was to be—

'Sorry—

'Perhaps if someone comes down here to have a—?'

**

Skuggs above, did Ruyfe cop the jug for it. No excuses or blame-shuffling. They interrogated me. I confessed I'd seen him throw it. 'It was me he threw it at. I didn't see where it went after it bounced off me, Sirs. I was on the floor, where he'd knocked me... and kicked me.

'He was disciplining me, Sirs. Somewhat ill of temper over some matter he imagined I was party to, Sirs, on a duty shift when I was not in the unit.'

They persisted, but I knew nothing. 'I didn't realise it had gone in there, until I checked – in case.'

'This is a hugely grave disciplinary matter, Drive Staff Bauer' the Enquiry Team said, in the most serious tone imaginable, 'and it is only thanks to you...

So I received a commendation for diligence.

And he got the push – endangering the ship, rendering a vessel of war temporarily out of commission, and thus hugely vulnerable to the enemy. Out here, *The Push* means exactly that – out the airlock.

I blew him the slightest of pouty-kisses as he was escorted past the official witness line-up, which included me. 'Bye, Rayffy,' I didn't dare smile.

The thing is, I'm the one who has to go in the ion shaft to fetch the offending pad out. It's not risky. Normally, I lock the drive controls, and key them to my own code, so nobody else can switch the units on while I'm down the shaft for routine cleaning or nozzle exchange.

At the moment, however, the power unit is still locked in active-live mode – ready warmed-up; instant action; Red Status Only Mode. That was the fault that Randy Ruyfe had come to blame me about – but it was Jayo Slazz who'd been on duty then. He was my only chief and the only other crew member in Number Three, with staff levels so decimated just now. But he hadn't come back for his shift, and couldn't be found anywhere aboard. Which left me covering for a double slot.

I didn't know what was up with Jayo, although he'd been depressed about the way the war was going around his home planet. Maybe he'd done something silly, like deserting at the overnight launch-call.

The downside is that, without him, there's nobody else qualified to do the job.

He must have deliberately code-locked the active-live control module. So had he then self-airlocked? Or has he secreted himself away, waiting for the whole ship to self-smithereen?

Me and Jayo had been a bit spanners-at-dawn at times when he'd been a randy flugger on a few take-overs and joint shifts and I hadn't played. But I couldn't really imagine him hiding out in a cubby somewhere just to inconvenience me. No... self-airlocking over home-planet despair seemed more likely.

Whatever, if I survive that long, the jammed key setting is something to tackle when I've checked the manual on what order to do the resetting in.

But, right now, I have to retrieve that keypad. I need to slide down the shaft, knowing the safety off-keys aren't working; and there's a pair of irate-looking officers manning the consoles and controls. I bet they're fluggered off about Randy Ruyfe being vacced – they look vacant enough to be his bed-bags.

This job should take me three minutes max, in and out. But it'd be so easy for one of them to touch the Live Drive pad. Just for one second. That'd be enough to fry me and chute the charring out the exhaust.

So, untrusting me, I've set a timer code on the emergency override for all four drive units. If I get instant-baked down there, I won't be able to cancel it within twelve minutes, will I?

In which case, this ship is heading for the Pit at an ever-building drive spin. It's anyone's guess how long it would take to overheat, and erupt in a cosmic fireball.

Hi Ho, here I go. Head-first down the shaft. Just another routine shift aboard the Space Navy Destroyer "All for One", hmm?

DO YOU HEAR WHAT I HEAR?

'Do you hear what I hear?'

Shipps to Shika! That made me jump. From somewhere behind me. Very close. Heart coming back to its right place, I turned. A touch awkward in a suit with all the connections, plus hefting an arm-sized adjuster-wench.

It was the Corrite, the alien from the ruling breed round here in the Grappolo Cluster.

What's it doing here? This my place. The cheek of it – muscling in on my rockball. Flugging nuisances they are – causing bother, interfering... Okay, so I'm only a one-woman op with my own little ship and drill rig, on this public-property asteroid out past Ayven. But it's my exclusive right to be here because I am "First and Established". Nobody else. Even a Corrite, with all their rules and regs and superior arrogance, can't come trying to move me on.

Sure, anybody can prospect such bodies, it's just that most won't, not on quick-spinners like JG-66-606. It rotates at such a speed that it's dangerous to land, and difficult to stay on. But I've been surveying and small-scale mining here for over a hundred days – which gives me all the rights. He shouldn't be here.

If anybody pays a visit, it's etiquette to apologise, and explain their reason of arrival. Not just turn up and start doing your own exploring, like this Corrite had done – five days now, he's been here. Not a word to me, on *my* rock; he's the Trespasser. Not that I've seen him doing any mining or sampling so far. He just wanders round, looking lost.

I call him "he" because most of them are what passes for males, most of the time. It's all a matter of season and age, I gather. Haven't delved. Don't intend to.

Introduces himself like that, 'Do you hear what I hear?' What kind of intro is that? The only two entities on the whole astral body and he comes sneaking up on me while I'm in my suit, up to my nipples in grease guns and a drill-bit change. That may not sound much, but it's a CrustBuster 5-Rotator Offset Cormoro drillhead that weighs as much as me, leaks hydro-fluid like an incontinent truffalo, and needs four hands to tighten all the bolts and blots at once. So this Corrite chooses to scare five turds out of me while I'm wrestling with that, and doesn't even offer to lend me a couple of hands – it's not like he doesn't have plenty to spare.

I ignored him for a mome – just – had – to – get – that tightened… Yes, Right. Wipe off.

Huh, Corries. They imagine they own everything, think they're superior shuggers. They are, actually. Mentally and physically. Philosophically, too, it's reckoned, believing they're nearer my god to them. Most times, they push it a bit, lord it over we mere humans, but it's part of their superiority not to be too common and obvious about it. They've even been known to take whole colonies of humans under their wings – almost literally. Or help with technical developments – advice, directions, and the like. Bit patronising, that; and that's not a trait of a superior being.

He – Now I think about it, I think they class themselves as "he" when they look like that – a sort of purply-green and more rigid antennae. It seems to vary, although it's not like I mix with them. Ever. What? Me and superior beings? Bar Servers are the most superior beings I ever encounter. Them, I worship.

Finished for the mo, I left off the drill-head exchange, with an impatient snort. They get the meaning of that kind of reaction from us. Not that it makes any odds to them; they understand us too well. It's one of the reasons they look down on us.

'Do I hear what?' I wiped the thickest of the grease off my gloves, and tried to listen through the intermittent silence, hum and faint tickerings that were the permanent background to in-suit communications. Apart from that, I was distantly aware of the tickle background of my air and heat meters, and very faint static. Plus him, suddenly bursting in on my concentration with this autovoice translation that sounds like a skidcab on cobbles.

I touched the mute dampener

'Hear what?' I repeated, clicking onto my Hold pattern for the Cormoro unit in case this was going to take more than ten seconds.

'And where the uff-chuff are you?' He was moving round like he was doing the Watermen's Waltz.

'Did you hear it?'

Uff! He was getting boring – my first ever close-up conversation with a Corrite and I'm uffed-off already. They're supposed to be stimulating, spirit-lifting. But this one? Interrupting my survey analysis in the final stage – looking promising too – half-a-dozen serious traces on rare-rock minerals and metallics. Uff uff uff, I'm inward-chundering.

'There. Again. Do you hear it?'

I moved slowly away from my porta-vey and listened – raised the in-audio reception on my suit, and turned round, head waving slowly to pick up extro-sounds better.

'No... nothing...' I looked at the Corrite; really close behind me – just appeared from nowhere. Ufferty! I never been so close to one – intimidating or what? Practically intimate. He only had a head-globe for the air – no suit, just, like normalish what I think are clothes – slack jacket cover like an embroidered waistcoat with gaps for the arm-clusters, and the wing casings – wow, they really do have them. No dress sense, though.

'Hush.' It spoke. 'Be still. Listen.'

Uff-it. Bossy Bollooger or what? He's making more noise than me, but, ever-obedient, I listened. *What am I listening for? Do they fart musically? Is this a special occasion melodious de-gassing? Or he does a terrific line in stomach rumbles?*

Stupid question in the first place – of course I don't hear what he does. His auditory sensors are pan-surface with deep-core basal processing organs – their whole skin-shell collects sounds. So Shipps-alone knows what they hear. I've no idea what *I'm* listening to most of the time, especially when a) working, and b) in Kaylee's Sozzle-Bar.

'There!'

I strained... Waiting. *There's something.* I strained and tried not to breathe. *Yes, something...* 'Hey, maybe. Like a high soft keening sound – bit like Ghosty Greta? That what you mean?'

He seemed to hesitate. I imagined he sniffed at my analysis and description. 'Yes.'

I was still striving to hear better. Like trying to tune in, now I know what range I'm listening for specifically. 'Hmm, yes, perhaps. I'm getting it more clearly.

Modulating? Similar to that Jiuka music they're into somewhere out Kohyu way?'

The Corry looked at me with about half of its eye clusters. 'I believe it is the true sound of the fabled H'yods.'

'H'yods? Yes, right.' *So you're trying to baffle me?*

'A higher being? One of The Gods?' He acted like I should know all about it, but personally, I never heard of them before. I mean, I scarcely heard much about the Corries; now here I am practically chatting with one about what sounds like his religion. He just heard his Maker and Master or something. Wanting me to verify it. *Sure, like that's gonna happen.*

Except, we both stayed still and listened, and I'm saying, 'Yes. Hear that? I'm getting it now.'

'No, I'm losing it...' His top antennae quivered and waved.

'Hush, then, Corry. Retune.' I waved a hand towards his anty-nest. He did, too, but I think it was dismissive, not quietening.

So we both stood there on this flat rock-patch in all the landslide jumble of boulders I'd been investigating. We listened to the undulating cadences – high and weird, fluctuating as if with the wind through the stars. Like you might imagine a cemetery of benign ghosts having a pray-in.

The sound was fading. I was losing it.

'It is a far higher form of being than either of us, Humo. We have legends and myths of our people hearing them on occasion, sometimes divining meaning within their sounds. But none has been able to discern any clarity of meaning. To us, they are The Gods.'

'I thought I was getting some kind of pattern among the sounds; and where there's pattern, there's meaning.' I don't think he was listening to me very much, but I carried on, 'I'm possibly hearing them more clearly than you can – with the different auditory systems we have.'

If I'd known what pensive looked like with the Corrites, he probably looked it. 'Can you describe the sound as you heard it?' he asked me. 'Mimic it, perhaps?'

'Eh? You haven't heard my singing voice,' I told him, blushing at the memory of last time in the Miners' Arms on Kalèdas. But he seemed keen, as though it could be some divine revelation – a window to the words of the Gods – some mystic insight. So I coughed a couple of times. 'No, that's not it,' I hastened to assure him, and tried to wail and keen, feeling ridiculous. I realised there was almost a rhythm... a kind of hoyluka tune that rose and fell.

The Corrite simply stood and listened to me. It was embarrassing. 'You heard that?' he asked me.

'Well, something of that nature, like translating from insectal Yappano into Terras by way of Stego IV.'

'A Humo interpretation?'

I shrugged, but in a suit, he couldn't have seen that. 'Actually,' I thought about it. 'Trying to reproduce it there, I'm wondering if there really is some discernible meaning to it – questioning, perhaps. As if it's wondering. About us, maybe?'

Another day of listening...
  We combine our understanding, me and the Corrite.
  We interpret and compare what we each hear.

'We've made Contact!' I suggested to him, but he was quiet about the idea.

One time, the sounds felt like a response to the noise I'd been wooing and wailing. So I tried to echo it back, and it changed again and I copied again, and stuck a sort of questioning tone on the end. Corry was catching some of it, and believing his prayer was being answered in oblique form; a reply edging around the same thoughts. Coincidence? Mere echoing? Or a direct response? We didn't know… Corry hoped and believed that it was the answer to his religious dreams.

He's totally joy-filled about it – in touch with his god… H'jod.

He didn't listen, so much as allow his beliefs to whisper the meanings. I watched him a couple of times… No, he wasn't listening carefully. I could discern details in the sounds that might contain real meanings in there, like words or tone of voice do for us. But Corry was only hearing what his religion wanted to hear… what his latest prayers had demanded, begged or worshipped for.

I thought I was doing it more open-mindedly, from the little I knew of music – I'm pretty eclectic in my musical tastes and usually have my musipad close at hand.

I was racking my brain to divine any recognisable meanings from it. My human ears probably heard it in a totally different way from Corry's. Plus, my brain was perhaps pre-tuned to these kinds of sounds; they do have parallels with the Jiuko modulations – I'm increasingly noticing similarities. *Must have some meaning I suppose, or neither the Jiuko performers or the H'jod would do it.*

Me and Corry were getting on well, almost like equals notching in together. I was hearing better than him, and relaying to him, and he was translating it all in terms of Corrite religio beliefs...

It was uffing awesome, and I thought I was coming to understand oddments and repetitions in the sounds, and perhaps something of their meanings without the religion to distort them. More and more, I've attempted to croon and ululate back to them, wherever they are. Somewhere all around us, I think. I was totally embarrassed about that the first few times, but Corry seemed to accept it as normal, so I got into the flow of it. And he listened and translated to his own beliefs.

'They seem to be concentrated in some places, as though diffuse beings with almost a corporeal core,' I suggested, but I don't think Corrie wanted to think of them as having any reality of presence; just to be ethereal God-is-Everywhere Beings.

'But Corry, it's something great... wonderful. The thoughts I'm getting, of reasoning beings. Sure, they're godlike to us, but it's not how they think of themselves. I get more of a feeling that they crave interstellar companionship, minds to exchange ideas with, knowledge to share, grow together. They want to communicate.'

He fluffed-up, not wishing to know, and cut the link. So I carried on – stuff the mining – doing my throat-yowling and eye-ball-rotating stuff, and they were answering! Really, like we were on the same wave-length. I mean, I was so pleased; never done anything like this before. More than a modicum awed that I was in sort-of contact with some unknown beings – aliens without much physical form. It felt like they were delighted – been looking for meaningful contact for millennia.

I had the impression of more of them, crowding around me, eager. Then settling – as if channelling their efforts through one calm voice... and we were flugging talking to each other – practically!

I'm wondering, most sessions, what to sing-think about; such as what they do all day... what I do... where they live... are they just visiting this rockball? What's their opinion of the dodgefall series this year? or Robinka music? Equal rights for pre-natal pitrins?

I'm getting better by the day, with glimpses of other places and beings. And even an inkling of different aromas! Perhaps a strange taste in my mouth, and I tried to imagine and ululate about one of my favourite dishes – salmonica with marmine sauce. I guess it's something you love or hate – their response was a bit ambivalent, so I imagine they got it pretty accurately. I tried to envision my home and family, and to project images and feelings across to them. I think they're getting something from it, because they renewed their imaging. And the sounds changed in tempo and melodies... whatever... I don't know. Intensity and complexity, perhaps. I had the idea they wanted to know what the drilling equipment was, so I started up the big Comoro CrustBuster. Boy – that had 'em skittling away for a time, then coming nosying back.

I'm real excited about it, and thinking about trying to get pics on the trivid for them, or doing drawings and representations, and working up to writing things down, or working out a code – like binary language – and some way they might operate something solid, or affect the electronics... Endless possibilities...

My mind is abuzz with this. Where do they want to take me in their images? in their minds? What can we teach each other?

But Corry still re-interprets everything I say. The little he hears himself, is all in terms of his re-awakening ancient belief system. In his eyes, his whole religious edifice is confirmed by this wondrous appearance of his gods... beings to blindly worship and bow to.

Do I hear what you hear? Oh, no – I hear so much more.

ABOUT THE AUTHOR

Trevor is a Nottinghamshire, UK writer. His short stories and poems have frequently won competitions. He has appeared on television discussing local matters, and his weather photographs are a regular background on the BBC weather forecasts.

As well as short stories – Sci-fi and otherwise – he has published many reader-friendly books and articles, mostly about volcanoes around the world, and dinosaur footprints on Yorkshire's Jurassic coast.

He spent fourteen years at the classroom chalkface; sixteen as headteacher of a special school; and sixteen as an Ofsted school inspector to round it off. Chris, his teacher wife jokes that it was a time of "Sleeping with the Enemy".

In the 1980s, his Ph.D. research pioneered the use of computers in the education of children with profound learning difficulties.

Now retired, he writes and walks; curses his computers and loves his wife and the cat.

Log on to the website @ https://www.sci-fi-author.com/
Or try Amazon - Trevor Watts - sci-fi
Facebook @ Trevor Watts – Creative Imagination

BY THE SAME AUTHOR

OF OTHER TIMES AND SPACES

The Giant Anthology – 460 pages with 39 tales of here and now, and the futures that await us.

If you were spying on another planet, would you do any better than Dicky and Miriam in the snappy two-pager "Air Sacs and Frilly Bits".

Could you live among the laughs and lovers of "I'm a Squumaid"? Or cope with the heartache of "The Twelve Days of Crystal-Ammas"?

In the novella-length "The Colonist", how could anyone fault Davvy's actions in setting up Hill Six-Four-Six with a party of Highraff refugee women and children?

How might you cope in class with the all-knowing "Thank you, Mellissa" and her little yellow ducks?

AMAZON 5* READER REVIEWS
— "Sci-fi at its most original"
— "Absolutely excellent, equal with anything I have read in the genre, including all the old masters when I was a kid."
— "Great entertainment and good stories from start to finish."
— "A sci-fi feast – I highly recommend it."

The New-Classic Sci-Fi Series

Zero 9-4 Book 1 in the New-Classic Series of Sci-Fi from the Lighter Side.

AMAZON 5* READER REVIEWS

"Loved the sheer variety on offer."

"A great book of short stories to delight any sci-fi reader's palette."

"Go on, give yourself a treat."

"More than 20 stories – loved every one."

- Does Cleanup foretell the future of humanity? Or is it in the hands of the scientists who believe the key to space-time manipulation is Zero 9-4? Or is They Call the Wind Pariah a premonition of our fate in the grip of the Corona virus?
- Are the aliens already among us in Betty? Or in the fire pit of Kalai Alaa?
- Dare you immerse yourself in the laughs and trials to come in It isn't easy Being a Hero, or Holes aren't my Thing?
- Are you prepared to join the war of the alien genders in Kjid, or Typical Man?

ORBITAL SPAM

Book 2 in the New-Classic Series of Sci-Fi from the Lighter Side.
AMAZON READER REVIEWS
"A great selection"
"A heads up on this third one I've read by this author"
"My kind of real characters – I get their humour and dilemmas and problems and solutions – or failures, sometimes."

- What would you do if you suspect your ship's been dumped in the Orbital Spam folder?
- Is there anything you can you do when the Great Pondkeeper up in the sky decides to call time?
- When a trail of disembodied footprints heads straight for you across the wet concrete in Self-Levelling, how do you respond?
- Would you answer the Prasap1 call?

These 20+ tales will alter your view of the future. The illustrations will brighten a boring wait at the space-port, or leisurely evening in orbit. Plus one poem: the beautiful, mysterious and stranded child – Mirador.

In his welcoming speech at the Xaatan Peace Conference, the Galactic High Commissioner described this book as, "The most entertaining read I've had in seven millennia... a great step forward for humanity."

TERMINAL SPACE

Book 3 in the New-Classic Series.
READER REVIEWS

"5* because it's basically the best sci-fi I've read for years."

"Surprised I was so taken up with these stories – Excellent."

"Completely absorbed in some of these situations – the atmosphere and the so-believable characters."

Twenty+ terrific Sci-Fi stories from the here and now and maybe-then, with illustrations.

- When Prisoner 296 is sent to carry out repairs in the Khuk spaceport's entrance tunnel at rush hour, will he find out why it's known as The Terminal Space?
- What on Earth can the alien do when he's stuck in traffic and going to miss his spaceship home?
- Could it be you who writes the heartfelt plea to Agony Aunt, Maar'juh'rih?
- If it depended on you, would there Always be an England?
- When it comes to that vital First Contact moment, would your first message be the same as the one that Polly settled on?

As Princess Porkyu said at the Cygnus Arms in 2929, "Laugh or catch your breath; shed a tear, or cheer them on, you'll immerse yourself with these souls of the universe."

THE FRACTUS PROJECT
Book 4 in the New-Classic Sci-Fi Series

20+ intimate sci-fi stories from the heights and depths of the fractal universe.

- Morris was desperate for Fame, but *this?*
- How can Mz Dainty possibly pass her space pilot driving test in the midst of so much chaos in the space terminal at rush hour?
- Will Sayida's radical change to the Fractus Project resurrect the near extinct human race?
- You have three minutes. Can you call the right shot when the enemy's High Space Drifter comes barrelling towards you?
- You have a choice; after all, you're the new Queen. Why would you choose The Little One on the End?
- The members of The Jolly Small Club don't always get on spiffingly well together. But when it comes to the new member…

EARLY REVIEWS of the New-Classic Series

"Highly recommend this one. It's absolutely excellent."
"A sci-fi feast… equal with anything I've read in the genre."
"So funny, and some real heart-stoppers, too.'
"Great entertainment… a refreshing change."
"What an eye-opener; the book, and the author."

NON-SCI-FI

Twists & Turns

Book 1 in the Odds, Sods and Surprises Series of Short Stories

"Superb stories."
"Such different situations, characters and moods."
"Very, very readable…"
"This book lifted my spirit."
"Compelling gems – whether light, funny or sombre, they are all rewarding and totally absorbing."
"There's nothing routine here."

- Could you live up to a Category Four Name?
- Baksheesh Bill could save the life of the enemy fighter pilot, but will he?
- Can she answer the ultimate question on Quiz Night?
- The *Prim* Reaper? Who are you kidding?
- It's the most expensive thing in the place – Please! Not my Mirror!
- Finally, The Truth – The Ten Command Moments
- You really shouldn't throw people around in glass houses

Roads Less Travelled
The Odds, Sods and Surprises Series
Book 2

Thirty terrific tales to delight or horrify anyone who uses or abuses the highways and byways, tracks and trails around the world.

****

- Why was the M42 closed that day?
- How many more times will the bride have to go round again?
- Some nights in Canada are so much colder than others, aren't they?
- Driving The Causeway as the tide comes in might seem risky, but...
- What's next on the menu at the Brass Kettle Diner, Tucson South?
- What would your therapist tell *you?*
- Will Sat-Nav Sadie take you on the full Australian tour?

****

Previewers –

"I've laughed, groaned and been shocked in equal measure."

"I'm sitting here going, *No, don't do it!* Or, *Yesss, get in there.* Really involving stuff."

"So funny I was reading passages out loud to my husband."

Other Writers

"Absolute classics among travel stories."

"Brilliant – such humour, justice and tragedy in everyday driving situations."

BOOKS TO COME

A FEW NOTES

Purely because I like the sound of my own keyboard, I thought I'd finish up by saying – there's no telling where stories are going to come from. The most common sources of stories are:

1.

Almost daily walks around Brinsley and surrounding villages, with a mind freed-up from the computer;

2.

Soaking in the bath with only a navel to contemplate;

3.

Sitting in the afternoon summer sun, in the garden, by the ponds, with a shandy to set the biro blazing across the page;

4.

Sitting in my car in a car park because I've arrived somewhere early for an appointment, and they won't let me in.

---oOo---

"Experience" came to me when I was in hospital in early 21 with a suspected stroke, and two attending doctors were introduced to me as joining the neurology team "for experience".

"It's in mi drawers" began at an antique fair at Newark, Notts, England. There was a chest of drawers that you'd chuck out your garage, and they wanted £800 for it! And I said, 'There must be a secret compartment hiding something pretty wonderful to make it worth more than its weight in firewood.'

"I'm working on that" is what the plumber always used to say when someone pointed out his latest leak, drip or clanking pipework.

"A will of her own" was someone I used to know who did whatever she fancied, and never had a care for the consequences for anyone else.

"The Secret of Vondur'Eye" arose from a police drama on TV, in which the hero-type detectives insisted on asking the most stupid questions imaginable, instead of the supremely obviously ones. I stopped watching that series.

"Coupla Yumans" – the situation was in the vet in Eastwood, Notts, when I saw an old friend, me with my cats, and he with a pair of dwarf lop rabbits peering up at me from a Morrison's bag-for-life, rescued from an uncaring family (the rabbits, not the bag).

"Scabby" is adapted from a chapter in Book One "Discovery" of the "A Wisp of Stars" trilogy.

"Survive the Night" began from the sight of a rusted, smashed-up bus in a ravine in the Dolomites, Italy. It grew as my imagination wandered.

"All for One" was inspired by an inspection team I briefly worked with, all working for and against each other in equal measure.

"Shimmer" is the sequel to "The Tangerine Affair" in The Fractus Project, although this one was written first, based on a persistent patch of heat haze on the beach at Skegness.

"Do you hear what I hear?" comes from the song of the same name (my favourite version is by the Harry Simeone Chorale). I just turned it round a little.

New-Classic Sci-Fi

Printed in Great Britain
by Amazon